C4 488900 00 59

D0492685

KEMP'S LAST CASE

The Lennox Kemp series by M. R. D. Meek

* *available from Severn House*

KEMP'S LAST CASE

M. R. D. Meek

This first world edition published in Great Britain 2004 by
SEVERN HOUSE PUBLISHERS LTD of
9–15 High Street, Sutton, Surrey SM1 1DF.
This first world edition published in the USA 2004 by
SEVERN HOUSE PUBLISHERS INC of
595 Madison Avenue, New York, N.Y. 10022.

British Library Cataloguing in Publication Data

Meek, M. R. D.
    Kemp's last case. - (A Lennox Kemp mystery)
    1.   Kemp, Lennox (Fictitious character) - Fiction
    2.   Lawyers - Fiction
    3.   Detective and mystery stories
    I.   Title
    823.9'14 [F]

    ISBN 0-7278-6124-7

Typeset by Palimpsest Book Produ
Polmont, Stirlingshire, Scotland.
Printed and bound in Great Britain
MPG Books Ltd., Bodmin, Cornwa

One

The stairs looked as if they would creak, the wood was seamed and cracked like old leather, and indeed when Kemp reached the third step there was a groan of protest under his foot. That's probably the first sound heard up here in years, he thought as he opened the first of the attic doors. The room was bare, surprisingly light as the sun shone in through uncurtained windows, and the only furniture an iron bedstead and a tiny cottage-style dressing-table. One of the maids would have slept here, and in her day might have stared out across wide parkland studded with trees, now Newtown's finest council estate.

There was a musty smell, not of uncleanliness though with a hint of mice. He left the door open and went into the second room. He had to put his shoulder to the door; we don't want visitors, the place told him, and he felt like apologizing for his presence, explaining to the watching walls that he had a right to be there.

The second room had gone the way of most attics – used as a repository for unwanted objects from below. There were broken chairs that had awaited mending for too long, an old sofa showing the stuff it was made of, a good mahogany sideboard let down by a lame foot, a tall pier glass hiding its blotched face in a dark corner. But in the centre there stood a large rolltop desk which looked both dignified and undamaged. It still held to the idea that it had a purpose, and as if asking to be put to the test a bunch of keys hung

1

from the lock. Keys and the objects they can open were irresistible to one of Kemp's inquisitive nature, and in spite of the cloud of dust which rose up into a shaft of sunlight he rolled back the lid easily enough. Nothing in the pigeon-holes, and on the velvety writing-pad only a scatter of paper clips and pencil stubs. He closed the lid, and tried the three drawers. Some force was necessary, for the heat of many summers and the damp of winters had warped the wood.

There was little to reward his efforts; a packet of yellowed paper and envelopes in the top one, a bundle of old news-papers in the second, and in the bottom drawer some three or four dusty notebooks jumbled up in a corner.

Kemp picked up one of the books at random. It was a diary bearing the logo of a pharmaceutical company, its name now merged and lost in a larger global concern. He looked at the date – it was twenty years ago, just about the time when he had himself arrived in Newtown.

Of course, these would be the working notebooks of Dr Enid Ayre. This had been her house and when she died she had left it to Florrie Watts, the housekeeper who had faith-fully dusted her furniture and scrubbed the surgery floor for as long as anyone in Newtown could remember, and who was now herself deceased.

Kemp knew all about Florence Watts for, although secre-tive in her ways, she had been voluble when making her will in his office a few years ago.

'I've got no one,' she'd said, flouncing into his client's chair. The Victorian word had come to his mind then for Florrie wore great skirts down to her ankles and made of some stiff material that rustled when she walked. 'So it's all to go to them charities, the ones Dr Ayre liked, she being medical. She'd no family neither, that's why she says to me: "Florrie, I'm leaving you Warristoun House because I know you'll look after it and not see it go to ruin . . ." There were folks then telling me to sell it and get a bungalow – daft idea, as if I would! When I'm gone, well, that's different. But it's all I've got, the house, and the bit of money she left me to take care of it. That goes when I go, Mr Kemp, like she told me . . .'

He had explained that it was an annuity and would die with her. She had asked him to be an executor, and was satisfied that either he or one of the other partners in his firm would carry out that duty. And here he was up in the attics, doing just that.

He'd seen Florrie from time to time in the town and always greeted her although she would only give him a restrained nod of the head as if she'd no wish to take it further – a common feature he'd found in people whose wills were carefully filed away at Gillorns, they would not wish to be reminded perhaps of their inevitable end . . .

He'd been told that Florrie had fallen and broken her pelvis, and when taken into the district hospital and away from her beloved Warristoun House she had faded, and given up hope. Visiting neighbours talked of her woes and worries. 'More concerned as to who's polishing the brasses than about her own bones,' they said, and wondered why she'd not be fed up with the place by now after all those years she'd spent looking after it. But some remembered that Florrie Watts had grown up in service, and would have taken it as her duty to keep the house as it had always been even when there was no one but herself to see it.

But not up here, thought Kemp. Her old legs hadn't managed those stairs for years. She'd told him that Dr Ayre left her all the furniture, but he remembered her saying there'd be no use for what had been in the surgery after what she called 'them medical officials' had removed all the patients' files and such stuff from the office. The rolltop desk she might look on as furniture but it wasn't something she could bring herself to use, so she'd had it removed to the attic.

It would soon have to go on another journey, to the auction rooms, where it could fetch a decent price – it was a beauty of its kind. But, first, Dr Ayre's diaries would have to be disposed of. Kemp looked round the attic and the relics of Edwardian and Victorian taste stared back at him without offer of help. Oh, where are all those ubiquitous plastic bags when we need them? He would have to make do with wrapping the little books in newspaper, and he'd seen some in the middle drawer.

Working on the bare floorboards he was making quite a tidy parcel when he caught sight of the date on one of the papers. Glancing at the others he found they were all from the one day – August 16th 1979 – two national dailies and Newtown's own *Gazette*.

The local paper had the biggest headline: 'Dominic's Body Found: a Mother's Anguish'. Despite other more world-shaking events, the story was still front-page in both the *Daily Telegraph* and the *Guardian*: 'Tragedy in Newtown. Police Find Boy's Body.' 'Now It's a Murder Hunt.'

Kemp spread the old newspapers out on the floor, the pages dry and stiff, the print faded but still readable. He remembered people talking about the case, which had happened a year before he had arrived in Newtown, but he had never known anything of the circumstances surrounding it, nor had he known any of the people concerned. The pages he'd found in the drawer of Dr Ayre's desk had been abstracted from the main newspapers – whoever had removed them had been only interested in this story of the murder of a boy in Newtown. Yet Kemp was sure there had been no sequel; when people mentioned the case it was only vaguely – almost as if it had never happened, or was over before it had any impact on the town. Yet as he skimmed quickly over the newsprint he realized that it had been a sensational story: a little boy, Dominic Fenwick, had gone missing, the agonized search by his mother and neighbours, then the police hunt and, finally and tragically, the discovery of his body.

The sun had moved across the windows and was hot on the back of his neck. He carefully folded the newspapers round the clutch of diaries, took a last look round the room and replaced the keys where he had found them in the lock of the desk. As he left he felt the dust settling back with soft sighs of relief, hoping to return to undisturbed sleep. It wouldn't be for long; he'd have the removal men in by the end of the week.

Back in his office in Gillorns on the square in the centre of Newtown he tumbled the notebooks out on his desk. There were six of them, covering the years 1974 to 1980, the year in which he understood Dr Ayre had retired. He made a note about the finding of the diaries in Florence Watts's probate file, secured them with elastic bands and popped them into a filing cabinet. They could wait. The pages from the newspapers, however, he put in his own briefcase. He would read them again later. In the meantime there were clients to see, a contract to draft and the mail to sign before he could indulge his curiosity further. But as he was leaving the office at six o'clock he had second thoughts, retrieved the diaries and and put them also in his case.

Two

'Now there's a terrible story,' said Mary Kemp, reading the newspaper reports over her husband's shoulder. She had brought their after-dinner coffee into the sitting room, where he had spread out the yellowed sheets on the table. 'That poor woman . . . Did you ever know her, Lennox?'

He shook his head. 'She must have left the district. There was no one in Fernley Cottage when I came to Newtown. You know where it is?'

'That lovely wee place just off the old village green? I've walked by it often. That's a great lane now for blackberries, and people go down it to reach the allotments. But the cottage itself, it's just a ruin, all boarded up and the garden gone wild . . . I've wondered who had it and why it's been left like that to go to waste. It must have been a fine garden once, there's cultivated plants run to seed and honeysuckle everywhere. It always seems to have the sun on it . . .' She broke off. 'Oh, it must have been from that garden he was taken . . .'

'Yes.'

The three newspaper reports all told the same story:

Dominic Fenwick, known to everyone as Rickie, aged seven, had been last seen by his mother Amy Fenwick playing in the garden of Fernley Cottage just after two o'clock on Monday August 13th 1979. The local police had been called at four o'clock, when he could not be traced anywhere in the neighbourhood, and a search was begun.

6

His body was found two days later stuffed into a hedgerow on the London Road, the other side of Newtown. He was still in the clothes he'd worn on the Monday. He had been strangled. He had been sexually assaulted.

Dave Cormac, the reporter for the *Gazette*, had managed to obtain a few interviews. The head teacher of Oldgreen Primary School described Rickie Fenwick as 'a very bright boy, very popular with his fellows, fond of games and dressing-up.' She warned Cormac not to try and talk to the other pupils, who were devastated. Mrs Amy Fenwick, a widow, was being consoled by relatives. Detective Inspector John Upshire said his men were terribly distressed by the finding of the body but that made them more than ever determined to catch the perpetrator of this brutal murder.

'The perp.,' remarked Mary. 'Someone must have been reading American fiction.'

'Well, it wasn't John Upshire, he was never a man for fiction . . . What I find strange is that the case wasn't being talked about when I came – it only happened the summer before . . .'

His voice trailed off, as did the thought – to be put away in that part of the mind marked 'not urgent, maybe think later' – as Mary murmured that it was time for the nine o'clock news. There was an ongoing Westminster scandal flapping wildly in the media to which both she and Kemp were temporarily addicted, as others might be to *Eastenders*, so he gathered up the old newspapers and stacked them with the diaries on a bookshelf near the fireplace, where they might well have remained for some time, simply having exchanged one dusty place for another, had Mary not remarked as she switched on the television: 'You could always ask him, John Upshire, I mean. It's been a while since you visited . . .'

The reproof in her tone outlasted the news, so that when

the pundits' nodding heads had faded from the screen Kemp
recalled his earlier curiosity.

'You're right. I've not been to see John for some time.
But we both know why.'

Mary laughed. 'Brenda is a wonderful woman, and at
least John'll not be lonely in his retirement, but she can be
trying . . .'

Superintendent John Upshire had recently retired from a
career which had begun in the Met and ended here in
Newtown to the very real regret of those members of the
local Force who had known him. He had been that rare
animal, a popular policeman, admired by colleagues and
liked even by the criminals he put away, who recognized
him as a fair opponent. Some of them reckoned he wasn't
that much cleverer than they were themselves, he was just
dogged in pursuit and had luck on his side; to John Upshire
all his villains had a stupid streak, all he had to do was find
and follow it.

As a widower for many years he had put up with the
lonely life, the difficulties of having any social life in a
town where everyone knew his job, the impossibility of
forming close relationships, particularly as he rose higher
in the hierarchy, but Upshire had accepted the burdens
without complaint. And now, in his later years, he had
married again.

As Mary had remarked, Brenda Furness was a wonderful
woman. She had been John Upshire's daily help for many
years, she herself was a widow and they were both of an
age. It must have seemed but a short step to ask her to 'live
in' – in short, to marry. What he perhaps had not realized
in simply inviting her to share his life was that she would
so thoroughly attempt to manage him, to make him over,
to do him good in every possible way, from choosing his
clothes to advising him on hair shampoo . . .

Brenda's rise in status and her predeliction for personal

as well as household management had extended to the Kemps as friends of her husband, and also in need of improvement.

'I'll not be having her teach me yet again how to mitre corners of bedlinen,' said Mary now, 'but that's no reason why you shouldn't just ring him up and ask him out for a drink.'

'He'd like that,' Kemp agreed. 'He's not really the solitary type, and he does miss the day-to-day busyness of the Force. It wasn't just work to him, it was his whole life . . . Of course, Brenda has done him a lot of good . . .'

'But you can sometimes get too much of a good thing,' said Mary, drily.

'Now, now, just because she finds you beyond help in the domestic stakes . . .'

'Not even a starter,' Mary agreed, with complacency. 'Do go and ring him. One thing about Brenda, she's no drinker apart from a safe wee sherry in the parlour with the six o'clock news, so she'll not want to be included in your invitation.'

'No, she'll just see it as an excuse for John to go down to the pub. When they got married she thought all policemen had a drink problem and here was one she'd save from the fire. John likes his pint well enough but he was always canny drinking it. The pub was a place of business for him, and those baby-blue eyes of his could scan a roomful of rogues when at their most boastful and vulnerable. I think it was only with me that he tended to relax, because I was neither colleague nor culprit, and he didn't have to mind his tongue. Looking back, I think we learned a lot from each other those evenings down at the Cabbage White . . .'

'She'll not let you take him there,' said Mary, 'he might meet up with some old cronies and come home paralysed. There's a perfectly decent old inn near where they now live, and the walk there and back will do your waistline good.'

9

'This women's doing-good thing seems to be catching,' complained Kemp as he picked up the phone, and dialled. It took him some minutes to fight his way through Brenda Upshire's high chirpy voice – like a blackbird on gin according to Mary – before he was allowed to speak to John himself, and arrange an early meeting. He did feel there was a certain pathos in the alacrity with which his suggestion of a quiet drink in the Old Inn at Ember was greeted.

'I wonder if I'll ever get like that,' he mused as he came back to the fire, 'glad to have a night out with an old pal, just to get away from the wife . . .'

He didn't wait to see the effect of his words, for Mary had a voice that could curdle milk if she had a mind to it. He simply scooped her up in his arms and carried her off to bed.

The Old Inn at Ember had gone through its gentrification stage some years back and had come through relatively unscathed – mainly through lack of finance and local interest – so the woodwork still retained the gouges and scratches of the years, the ringed beerstains of long ago, and a certain smell that hovered close to the yellow ceiling as evenings drew on, but at least the hard benches had gone, and there were cushioned seats. On those John Upshire and Lennox Kemp settled themselves in an alcove like animals that know their home ground.

'They don't serve a bad pint here,' Upshire acknowledged, putting down his tankard carefully on the table in front of him. Later he wouldn't bother being so careful; Brenda's training of him with a teacup only went so far. 'I like the place. Should come here more often . . .'

'And I should see you oftener,' said Kemp, understanding. He paused for a moment. 'I think about the old times, too . . . You and me, no one at home, talking over the business of the day . . .' He tried to keep his tone light, avoiding any sentiment.

The retired policeman's features were still cherubic, despite age, and now they creased in a grin. 'You want summat, Lennox, I know you . . . You didn't get me here just for the chat. Come on, what's bothering you?'

Best to be direct. 'There was a case in Newtown just before I got here. Would be in the summer of '79. Little boy went missing, then found murdered. Had lived with his mother, a Mrs Fenwick, over at Fernley Green.'

Upshire looked at him with bland, baby-blue eyes. 'You've been looking things up, haven't you?'

Kemp explained the circumstances, the finding of the old newspapers in Dr Ayre's desk. 'I just thought it curious that I didn't hear more about the case . . . What happened to it?'

'Dr Ayre, eh? Well, she did have an interest, of course. It's likely she kept the cuttings at the time, then they got left there. She was on the point of retiring, anyway . . .' He drained his pint. 'My turn, I think . . .' He set off to shoulder his way to the bar. It was surprising how many people greeted him: at one time they'd have given him a wide berth but now he was only a retired policeman their natural desire to be friendly overcame an equally natural suspicion that John Upshire might know too much about them or their families.

Back at the table, he said: 'You'd not hear about the Rickie Fenwick case because there wasn't anything much to hear about. We got the man who did it, and he died. That was all there was to it.'

'He died in police custody?'

'Now, now, Lennox, don't get carried away by the tabloids. Perce Cavendish died in the prison hospital of stomach cancer within a month of being arrested. End of case.'

Kemp thought for a moment. 'Any reason why Dr Ayre should keep those cuttings, John? How was she involved?'

'Cavendish tried to use her as his alibi for the afternoon when the boy was taken. It wasn't true, of course, but there was a long shot that the defence might have called her as a witness. But there never was a trial.' He sighed. 'A bad business, all round. Folks prefer to forget it . . .'

'Hence the silence?'

'You could say that. I was sorry for Amy Fenwick, and pleased when she was able to move away to relatives in London. And if you're going to ask if I was sorry for the bloke that did it, then don't . . .' He glared at Kemp to block any such try. 'From all accounts it wasn't an easy death, the man Cavendish's, but there wasn't a soul in Newtown would have wanted it otherwise. Not after what he'd done . . .'

'There was no doubt?'

Upshire's glance was withering. He took a long drink, and brought the tankard down hard on the table top. 'He was a no-good son of a bitch, called himself an actor out of the East End, a mere bit-player more like . . .' That's a quote from someone else, thought Kemp, too Shakespearean for John Upshire. 'And he was a practising paedophile before the papers made 'em popular . . .'

Kemp smiled uneasily. He had always found John Upshire to be a fair man, one not given to inconsiderate opinion. Bringing up the Fenwick case seemed to have touched a raw sore, perhaps because of the way it had ended, a nasty crime but no criminal tidily put away for it.

As if to soften his previous harsh words, John leant over and said, quietly: 'Don't get me wrong, Lennox, this wasn't just personal feeling on my part. All my men were horrified when the body was found. Tossed into a hawthorn hedge like thrown-away rubbish . . . his little socks stuffed in his mouth . . . Perce Cavendish was lucky to escape a lynching when they brought him in . . .'

'Cavendish?' Kemp queried. 'There was a Reverend

Cavendish out at Castleton Parish Church when I came to Newtown.'

Upshire snorted. 'No relation. Though Perce would have liked folk round here to think so. He took Cavendish for his stage name, thought it sounded more posh than his real one, which was plain Percy Scroggs . . .'

'Well, he wouldn't have got far with that on the London stage except maybe as a comedian. Was he a local himself?'

'No way. Came out here while resting between performances was the way he put it. Others said he'd had some kind of breakdown and came to the country to recover. Been here a few months and he's taken on at the school, helping out with poetry and drama, that kind of stuff. That's how he got to know the kids, and in particular, Rickie Fenwick. The little lad would've followed him anywhere . . .' John Upshire gazed down into his beer.

Kemp watched his face change; it was suddenly savage. It had nothing to do with the stuff he was drinking but a lot to do with pent-up feeling, bad memories and the ragged edge of something personal. Recognizing this, he went carefully.

'There must have been repercussions?'

'Oh, aye, plenty of those . . . Why'd we not got on to him sooner? . . . Why'd we not known we'd one of them here on our patch? . . . We got lambasted by the press . . .'

'Hindsight,' said Kemp, with sympathy, 'their prerogative in these cases. Of course they always know – after the event, and bring out the same old patter. Why didn't Social Services act? Why didn't the medicos recognize the symptoms? Why didn't the accountants spot fraud? The whole area of professional uncertainty is a fertile field for investigative journalism in the aftermath of crisis.'

John Upshire took a long drink, wiped his mouth with the back of his hand, and grinned. 'I could always count on you, Lennox, you'd have the words. It's what I cottoned on to back then, when we first met . . . Other lawyers I'd met, most of them were shit-scared of looking bad in court, shined their shoes but never their wits . . . You were different. You made sense of your clients' stories no matter how far-fetched. You worked for them . . .'

'Maybe because I'd once been down there with them in the lower depths,' said Kemp, lightly. His past relationship with John Upshire had engendered a mutual respect despite inevitable clashes when their professional interests were on opposing sides and some kind of justice had to be ground out in the space between.

'Well, no use looking back,' said Upshire, as if aware of a possible lapse into sentiment. 'I'm enjoying retirement. You should try it.'

'No chance.' Kemp snorted. 'Remember, I'm in the private sector. I'll never get a pension package like yours . . .' As he spoke, and the conversation drifted into more general terms, he realized that he had been sidestepped. John Upshire had not wished to be questioned further on the case of Dominic Fenwick, indeed he had been reluctant to speak of it from the start, and by now he had steered their talk so far from Kemp's original query it would have been in the worst possible taste to renew it.

They parted at the door of the pub on the best of terms, and with promises to make such meetings more regularly in the future, but as Kemp walked home he thought what a wily old bird Upshire still was; he had not lost that trick of seeming innocent while leading a suspect all round the houses, and tonight he had led Kemp well away from a subject with which he was not happy . . .

Three

The past had already thrown one tentacle out at Lennox Kemp but as if that was not enough to hold him, it now threw another.

'We have an invitation for dinner with the Sutherlands,' Mary informed him the next evening. 'Saturday week at eight o'clock.'

'Fine with me. Say thank you and yes, please . . .' Kemp didn't look up from his paper. James Sutherland had been retired some years now from the general practice he had run in Newtown but he and his wife, Marion, still gave good dinner parties.

'I already have . . . They're entertaining an old flame of yours . . .'

That brought Kemp's head up. 'Who?'

'Don't you mean, which one?'

'No, I don't. What I asked was, who?'

'She was a Lettice Warrender. You must have known her when she was all crisp and green . . .'

'Oh, come on, Lettice Warrender was never a flame, not even a flicker. She was nought but a kid . . .'

'H'm . . . big enough to be taken out by you to some fancy do at Courtenay Manor . . .'

Kemp looked at his wife suspiciously. 'Just what sort of nonsense has Jim Sutherland been talking?'

'Well, you know he has this kind of chuckle – one of the privileges of age, I daresay – which he uses as innuendo

15

when he has a bit of a gossip, and he loves gossip, particularly when he's talking to me about your past life in Newtown before I rescued you from it.'

'I can guess,' said Kemp, briskly. 'Sometimes I think he's surveyed my progress in the last twenty years as if he was writing the life of a modern Casanova . . .'

'He's not just a gossip, he's a very acute old man, and when he tells me something I take note. This Lettice, kid or no kid, she was rather a protégée of yours?'

Kemp got up, took Mary gently by the shoulders and pushed her into an armchair. 'Just tell me,' he said, 'exactly what Jim's been telling you.'

'Well,' said Mary, rather breathlessly, 'he said to tell you they had a surprise for you. An old flame, chuckle, chuckle, like I said, visiting from the States.'

Kemp frowned. 'Lettice Warrender? From the States?'

'Yes, from the States – and complete with husband called Tod Aumary, an eminent physician over here on a lecture tour. Jim even spelled his name for me as he said you'd remember him better under the name of Torvil. Well, I was losing the thread by then and got the giggles and had to ask if Dean was coming too. Jim only chuckled again and said that was the reason he'd changed his name to Tod, because otherwise he'd always be asked where Dean was and were they still skating . . .'

'Torvil Aumary? Good God . . . He was only a tender young medico when I knew him . . .' Kemp thought for a moment. 'You said he was Lettice Warrender's husband? Surely she didn't go and marry that cousin of hers?'

'I know nothing of any family relationship, only what Jim told me. It was he who put in the old flame bit, and said you'd once taken her on a binge out at Courtenay Manor. Isn't that the site of the new Adventure and Leisure Park the Council are trying to foist on us?'

'It was certainly not a binge. I very nearly lost my life

... Adventure and Leisure certainly sums up what those terrible twins, the Courtenays, stood for but they've been safely put away for years. They were the last relics of whatever gentry Newtown could boast of – and could well do without.'

'Weren't the Warrenders gentry too? I've heard the name about the town.'

'Of a lesser sort. All that lot, the Courtenays, the Cavendishes and the Warrenders, were out there on the rim twenty or so years ago, just holding on to their depleted estates by the skin of their teeth. Then along comes our expanding town and pushes them over the edge, and we have nice golf courses instead – and of course council houses and schools ... Castleton House where the Warrenders lived is now a business centre – which is ironic since Lettice's dad was possibly the most inept stockbroker in the City.'

'Well, I'm sure they were glad of the money.' Mary had no sentimental notions about the fate of local landowners. 'Explain this cousinship bit to me before I meet up with your old flame.'

As Kemp spoke about the people who had lived at Castleton House twenty years ago it was Lettice who came back to him the most vividly. She had been so young and vibrant, a small compact girl with bright hazel eyes, ready to challenge the world. In her own way she had already done so. She had veered off the path chosen for her by her mother (what a frightful snob Paula Warrender had been): as soon as she left Benenden – where she had known, but disliked, Venetia Courtenay – she refused the offer of a finishing school in Switzerland, and chose instead a degree in a local college and a lowly position in the Town Planning department of the Development Corporation, the moloch which was slowly devouring the Warrender lands. Kemp had admired her spirit, especially when she said, stoutly:

17

'I believe in what's going on here. Our lot had those acres by inheritance over hundreds of years, it's time for us to leave . . .'

'I wonder why on earth she married her cousin,' he said now. 'I did hear that her father, Lionel, was in some kind of trouble in the City – he was never cut out to be any kind of businessman, he should have stayed the small country squire.'

'You think she might have married this doctor chap to save the family fortunes?' Mary sniffed; she thought this the stuff of fairy tales. 'Was he attractive, this Torvil without the Dean?'

'Not to me . . . I thought he was an arrogant young pup, the turning of a medical student into a doctor seemed to be a lengthy process in Torvil's case but perhaps I was prejudiced. He and Lettice's brother, Roger, played a nasty trick on me once.'

'Tell me about it.'

Kemp did so but with some reluctance. With the hindsight of twenty years he recognized that the two young men may well have thought at the time that he was indeed trying to seduce their precious young Lettice, so freshly sprung out of the good earth – the salad image kept recurring. For the pair of them had set on Kemp one dark night and he'd taken quite a beating. Perhaps they thought they had reason . . . Kemp was surprised now to find that rancour remained with the memory. Mary heard its undercurrent.

'Well, I hope that doesn't reappear at Saturday's dinner party,' she said, briskly. 'Now, have I got it right? Lettice and Roger are the children of the shaky Lionel and snobbish Paula, so who is Torvil, now Tod?'

'He's the son of Paula's brother Richard Aumary, who married an American lady called Giselle. All I remember of her is that she had legs like a greyhound. Richard was also a doctor as his father had been before him. It looks as if the Aumary family had lost their lands much earlier and had the sense to diversify into a profession. I suppose originally they were Norman–French, so they might well have been the first noble family in the area, outclassing all the Cavendishes, Warrenders and Courtenays put together. I believe Richard Aumary went to the States, and perhaps Torvil followed him. It may well be that our National Health Service didn't give enough scope for his talents . . .'

'And he thought he'd do better going stateside. Didn't they call it the brain drain? Seems to have been successful in his case – Jim described Tod Aumary as eminent, and Jim's not given to overpraising his fellow doctors. Now, Lennox, I'm hoping you'll not be holding a grudge . . .'

'Of course not.' Kemp was indignant at the idea. 'It was a long time ago, and they were young.' Yet once the memory was in his mind it took a firmer grip. 'Besides, as I remember, it was brother Roger who was the more vicious . . .'

'Wouldn't he have looked slant at you if he thought you were after his sister?' said Mary, reasonably. 'You not being the respectable lawyer you are now with a good practice, an infant daughter and a wife above reproach.'

Kemp grinned at her fondly, and ruffled her short brown hair. 'Just a few years ago, Mary, you were hardly the New York Police Department's pin-up of the month – except under the wanted ads . . . Time and circumstance change people, and the way we look at them. You're right, of course, Torvil and Roger saw me then as an outsider, and a threat. The Law Society had only reluctantly re-admitted me after that embezzlement charge, and all Newtown had heard rumours . . . .'

It had been a sticky start for Kemp at Gillorns. His former practice over at Leatown on the other side of the county had crashed when his ex-wife Muriel had been addicted to gambling and set him a problem which he couldn't avoid.

Either she paid up the huge losses or got acid thrown in her face. He had taken the money from trust funds and sold up everything to replace it but the Law Society took a strict line; he spent six years out of his profession and only hard work and old Archie Gillorn's faith in him had allowed him to return to it. Looking back now at those early years, he could understand why he had never been exactly welcomed by the Warrenders at Castleton House – to them he was that rather shabby solicitor from the East End of London who spent a lot of his time among criminals. Hardly a decent suitor for their daughter, even had he been serious . . .

'I remember Lettice saying that Cousin Torvil meant to get to the top of the tree as the new breed of medic, computerized patients and healthy profits . . . It sounds as if he has done so, but I still wonder why she married him . . .'

'Well, just don't be speculating about it out loud when we meet them,' said Mary. 'You don't want to be bopped on the nose again. And keep your eyes off Lettice . . . You may have known her in her salad days but she's no longer on the menu as far as you're concerned. Anyway,' she reassured herself, 'even green girls tend to wilt over the years . . .'

Four

It was inevitable that the conversation at the Sutherlands' dinner table on Saturday night should veer towards the past for all the participants, Jim and Marion Sutherland, Lennox and the visitors from America, Dr Tod Aumary and his wife, Lettice, had more in common twenty years ago than they had now. Once present-day trivia had been got out of the way over drinks in the sitting room, each seemed to be drawn back, some eagerly, others with more reluctance, to their earlier lives.

The Sutherlands themselves might well have anticipated how the evening would go. When you invite guests who have been long away from the neighbourhood to meet people they knew earlier, then the talk would tend towards a certain nostalgia, and this was particularly so when those present were unlikely to meet in other circumstances. Tod and Lettice had lived in New York for the last twelve years, Tod returning to England only for professional reasons, Lettice not at all. As she explained to Kemp when he enquired about her parents, they had retired to Florida about the same time as she and Torvil married (she tended to call him that more and more as she talked of the past) and both Lionel and Paula had died there.

'I think Mother took to Florida better than Dad . . .' There was a certain wistfulness in her tone, and sadness in her eyes when she spoke about her father. 'He never really left England, you know, his idea of England, I mean . . . It was never the same for him after the crash . . .' She had told Kemp this while he sat beside her on the sofa before dinner, and no one else seemed to be listening. Kemp had nodded, but made no comment. She presumably assumed he had known that Lionel's firm had been hammered in the City, although actually all he'd heard had been rumours. He remembered that at the time he had been saddened; he'd liked Lionel, a countryman who should have stuck to his woods and fields instead of bargaining them away for a hollow, transient prosperity.

Lettice had gone out to the States with them, she said, and then, quite simply: 'When I was there, I married Torvil . . .' At this point her tête-à-tête with Kemp was interrupted by the move into the dining room, so with that plain statement Kemp had to be content – for the moment.

For Lennox Kemp the conversations over the dinner table flickered like a despairing light bulb, on and off, subjects he found of interest dying suddenly, others seeming too general, too banal, topics in yesterday's news . . . He wondered why he was not finding the company as congenial as he had expected and realized it was because he was so disappointed in Lettice Aumary. There she sat, opposite him now, the typical American matron, smartly dressed, a little plump, her manner the careful poise of one used to being out in a discerning society. Gone were all traits of the impulsive girl, the sudden gush of words, the quickness of breath and the eagerness with which Lettice had at one time pursued her arguments, given her youthful opinions. Now she seemed simply to be filling a place; the wife of this top physician, she would share his New York apartment, give dinner parties, be the perfect hostess and never deviate from correct behaviour . . . She was no longer the Lettice Warrender Kemp had known; her fire had gone out.

Suddenly he felt the need to challenge her. There was a pause in the talk, so he addressed her directly.

'And do you really like it over there in the States, Lettice?' The words came out more roughly than he'd intended, and she looked for the moment taken aback, but there was something of the old Lettice in the way she answered him.

'Of course, I like it. For all you hear to the contrary, New York is a pleasant place to live. I missed England at first but now, no, I wouldn't like to come back except for a break like this.' She turned from Kemp and spoke to Mary. 'Marion tells me you and Lennox have a little girl. How old is she?'

From the ensuing conversation, it was clear that the Aumarys had no family.

'We were just not fortunate,' said Lettice, simply. There was no regret in her voice, but Mary diplomatically dropped the subject, and returned to a discussion she had been having with Tod about various eccentric families she had known when nursing down on Long Island. Initially, he had been surprised to learn that Mary knew some of these illustrious people at all but she had made no secret of the fact that she had been employed in their great houses in a professional capacity. He found himself warming to this wife of Kemp's who had a sprightly manner and a surprisingly perceptive mind.

From across the table Kemp had been watching this bit of by-play while listening to Marion Sutherland on the subject of vandalism in the town square – a topic too threadbare already to withstand further weight of words. He had changed his opinion of Torvil Aumary and was quite prepared to call him Tod. He liked the way the physician was bending his ear to Mary, and had relaxed the somewhat starchy manner with which he had originally greeted the company. Perhaps he too had been nervous of renewed acquaintanceship with folk from his Newtown past. Then, as Kemp remembered him, he had been a rather bumptious young medico, arrogant in the assumption that six years of study had made him lord and master in the field of medicine.

Now he had achieved the gravitas proper to his profession, he had also become more likeable, and somehow – even to Kemp, who was prejudiced – more acceptable as a husband to Lettice. He also had to acknowledge that Tod Aumary was very good-looking. Perhaps Mary had been right in her feminine logic; it could be that Lettice had indeed been attracted by the outward appearance of her clever cousin – no more to it that that. Kemp, whose most fervent admirers had never gone further than to compare him to a worn but appealing teddy bear, sighed.

He was delighted then to hear Lettice break off her conversation with Jim Sutherland to make her own comment on Newtown's delinquent young: 'I'm sure you don't still watch them from your bed-sit above the builders' yard, Lennox. You were quick enough then to shut them out by closing those horrible folk-weave curtains of yours . . .'

Even Mary looked surprised; perhaps she hadn't quite expected such a return to what Kemp had warned her was Lettice's habit of saying whatever came into her head without thinking of the consequences. Kemp himself was inordinately pleased. The very mention of those awful curtains – which went with the flat and all its other sordid furnishings – had gone straight to his heart.

'Alas, dear Lettice, those days are over – we now live in surroundings more appropriate to our station . . . But thank you for remembering . . . I loved that flat, it was always like living on the edge of things . . .'

She just nodded, and turned away, but he thought there was a glimpse of the old impish girl in the half-smile she gave. He was satisfied; there was still the spark there of the Lettice he had once known, and had treasured in his memory. There had been something of an uncle-and-favourite niece relationship between them. When a boyfriend was away it was Kemp she would call on to take her to some function or other she was expected to attend –

including the affair at Courtenay Manor to which Jim Sutherland had alluded. Thinking of it now he was reminded to ask about her brother.

'Is Roger still in this country, or has he too crossed the Atlantic?'

It was Tod rather than his wife who answered. 'I'm afraid that Roger has been ill recently. We shall be seeing him later. Yes, he is still in London.'

Kemp made the conventional sound proper to hearing of illness, and ended with the hope that it was nothing serious. He did not greatly care; Roger Warrender had been an unplesant youth.

The talk round the table seemed to have taken a sudden dive into Marion's finely wrought raspberry pavlova at the mention of Roger's name. Everyone murmured appreciation as they lifted their spoons and Kemp's query went unanswered till Lettice spoke out sharply.

'It is serious. Roger has just gone into a rehabilitation clinic for the second time. He's an alcoholic.'

Neither of the Sutherlands said anything. The nature of Roger's illness was obviously not news to them.

Mary leaned across the table to Lettice. 'It is hard when it happens to one in your family,' she said, softly, 'but at least your brother has sought help. That is often the first step to recovery.'

Kemp recognized the look of Lettice's mouth, the firmly folded line of the lips. Like her mother, he thought. She has developed a hard streak.

But it was her husband who answered for her. 'We hope so. We hope so.' Like many doctors he tended to repeat himself as if to be sure the patient understood. He turned to Kemp. 'You'll remember that Roger went into the City at a particularly bad time – just months before his father's firm collapsed.'

Kemp had not remembered. When he knew Roger

Warrender, the young man was supposed to be studying for a business career. 'My son's up at Oxford,' he'd heard Paula say, without adding that the college he was attending was commercial rather than academic. If Roger had been a disappointment to his mother then, it seemed he had continued on this course. However, there seemed little one could say further on the subject, so Kemp simply complimented Marion on the crispness of her meringue and hoped the conversation might now take a turn for the better.

He would do what he could to help it along. 'You knew Dr Ayre, didn't you, Jim?' he asked his host. 'Her housekeeper has died and I have the task of sorting out the contents of Warristoun House.'

'I couldn't help but know Enid.' Jim chuckled. 'She was here when I came, and seemed old as the hills even then.'

'I liked her,' said Marion, 'and so did a lot of people. She may have been old-fashioned but I'm sure she did no harm.'

'That we know of. Sorry, perhaps I shouldn't have said that. Enid hadn't attended a medical course in years, never read her journals, so she was hardly likely to be au fait with the latest trends in medicine. But at least she'd the sense to refer her patients when she got stuck – though that didn't make her popular with the consultants, who were busy enough without having to look at every child with spots she sent along to them. That house now, Warristoun – didn't it belong to your family at one time, Lettice?' Jim didn't wait for an answer before asking Kemp if the house was already on the market.

'It will be. It was in the attic that I found some items of Dr Ayre's, and a bundle of old newspapers.'

Lettice glanced at him, and remarked to Mary, 'When Lennox used to get that expression on his face it meant he'd found something to set off his curiosity. What is it this time?'

Mary looked at her husband, who nodded. 'That murder in Newtown, the poor woman at Fernley Cottage who lost her little boy.'

'Good lord!' exclaimed Jim Sutherland. 'Amy Fenwick. I'd almost forgotten. Happened that hot summer. Weren't you here then?'

Kemp shook his head. 'I came the following year, and only heard about the case vaguely. Nobody was talking about it much.'

'They did at the time,' said Marion. 'The town got a lot of unwanted publicity. The man who did it, the man who killed the Fenwick boy, he died, didn't he?'

'He died of cancer.' Jim's voice was harsh. 'He may not have deserved to die like that, but he most certainly deserved to be put away for life. He'd had a history of sexual attacks on children, even before he came to Newtown. Perce Cavendish was a menace to society.'

'Was that his name?' Tod asked. 'All I remember is that the whole town seemed to be out scouring the countryside, and then there was an awful kind of blankness when the body was found. I must have been doing my stint as a registrar at the North Mid and you remember, darling . . .' He turned to his wife. '. . . I used to come out to your place whenever I had any time off – which wasn't often . . . God, the hours they expected us to work, it's a wonder we knew one end of a stethoscope from another!'

'It was no different in my day,' said Jim Sutherland, mildly. 'It was a kind of testing ground for your future in the profession, or cheap labour for the overworked hospitals – depends on your viewpoint. Anyway, it seems to have done you no harm, Torvil, you've made quite a name for yourself in America as I see from articles in the journals. Sorry . . . you must forgive an old man for using your old name – I can't think of you as Tod . . .'

'And I, for one, couldn't see any reason to change it,'

27

said Lettice, stiffly. 'It certainly wasn't my idea. My mother was shocked. She said Torvil was a perfectly good Aumary name, had been in the family for centuries.'

Kemp wondered if Paula Aumary had ever heard of Torvil and Dean – probably thought they were some of the common people one couldn't help seeing on the television. It was a pity that Lettice had grown so like her mother. Perhaps suitors had been discouraged by having tea at Castleton House and meeting Paula – he himself had found that experience unnerving.

But Lettice surprised him again. 'What sort of a price is Warristoun House likely to fetch, Lennox?' she asked him. He'd forgotten she had once been a small cog in the works of the Development Corporation's planning department.

'Oh, I'll leave that to the vagaries of the property market but it will be high, so the list of medical charites will benefit. The late Mrs Florrie Watts felt it her duty to carry out Dr Ayre's wishes, though she was under no legal obligation to do so.'

'I'm glad to hear it,' said Jim Sutherland. 'Dr Enid told me what she intended to do with the house, she felt that her old housekeeper would do the right thing . . . Dr Enid herself may have been a bit of a muddler and she should have retired a long time before she did, but her heart was in the right place.'

'And where else should it have been?' remarked Mary, lightly, so that everyone laughed. 'And maybe she just kept those old newspapers because they were concerned with Newtown – and she would think of herself as part of the place . . .'

Mary pouring the warm oil on troubled waters, thought Kemp, watching her, and indeed her words seemed to smooth the edginess which had crept into the conversation.

'I think you're probably right,' her host agreed. 'Dr Enid

did have a strong sense of belonging. She had only a small practice but she ran it single-handed . . .'

Tod asked if the patients had been shared among the other local practitioners when Dr Ayre retired.

'Well, some went to doctors out at Ember and we got the ones actually in Newtown itself. Dr Enid's patients were for the most part female and of an older generation.'

'And perverts like Perce Cavendish . . .' Lettice's interjection was shocking.

'How did you know he was her patient?' asked Kemp, filling up the silence which had fallen.

'He told me so himself . . . Oh, why is everybody pussyfooting round the subject? We all knew Perce . . . Even you, Torvil. It's nonsense to say you don't remember.'

Marion had been busying herself at the trolley with coffee cups and saucers. She made an unnecessary clatter. Her husband got up to help.

'Hey, there, Lettice . . .' Tod Aumary took an easy tone. 'Why're you having a go at me? I'd completely forgotten the whole thing. And I don't remember ever knowing this Perce Cavendish fellow . . .'

'We all knew him,' said Lettice, stubbornly. 'That play he got the school to do up on the Common. It was *A Midsummer Night's Dream*, or bits of it, he adapted it. You must remember. Rickie Fenwick was Puck . . .'

Her husband laughed. 'You, Lettice, have a terrific memory for the most trivial of events. All I remember about that summer was that it was hot and I was working myself to death at the North Mid. I certainly wouldn't have had the time for some piddling little play on your village green.'

Marion handed Kemp his coffee in silence. He shook his head at the sugar basin, and thought that Lettice needed rescuing; it wouldn't be the first time.

'Events that happened over twenty years ago are only a blur in my mind, and when I try to recall them, or the people involved, they tend to float away. If I never see those people again they've vanished for ever, or they've become distorted by other's opinion, or even my own imagination. Memory is illusive, not to be altogether trusted . . .'

Even as he was speaking, Kemp felt the words were pretentious. He might have used them to a witness unsure of his ground, but, damn it all, this was only a dinner party . . .

But Tod Aumary was quick to applaud. 'Well said. Very well said. My own opinion entirely . . . It's not only myself, I find it in my patients, their recollections never fully to be valid. And in your line of country too, in court for instance when even the best of us can be disorientated by the surroundings . . .' He went on to describe an occasion when he'd had to appear as an expert witness in a New York court-room . . .

It was interesting, and Tod told the story well, even as it ended with a joke against himself. The room warmed, liqueurs were produced and the Sutherlands relaxed with their guests – another dinner party brought to a successful conclusion – so that by the time taxis were called an atmosphere of some cordiality had been achieved. Even Lettice seemed to have thawed.

'I hope we shall see more of you while we are over,' she said to Kemp and Mary as they were leaving. 'We're in London. I'll give you a ring . . .'

'Will she, won't she . . .?' said Mary that night, brushing her hair at the dressing-table. 'She's a changeable lady, your Lettuce Leaf . . .'

'Didn't you like her?'

'She doesn't give one much chance to. She's so buttoned-up . . . Makes you wonder what'll pop out if the seams give . . .' She shivered.

'Are you cold? Shall I close the windows? It is autumn, after all . . .'

'Not that sort of cold. Rather the walking-over-the-grave kind. I honestly didn't like this evening's dinner party, Lennox. There was something wrong. Even the Sutherlands weren't at ease . . . As for Torvil . . . Well, he is good-looking, isn't he? Good-looking, clever and at the top of his profession . . . Who could wish for anything more. But his wife isn't happy . . .'

Mary found she was talking alone; her husband was asleep.

Five

'One thing I did find out from Marion-in-the-kitchen,' Mary told her husband the next day, running the words together to emphasize that Marion Sutherland might have two personas, and the one in the kitchen was more forthcoming.

'And what was that?'

'The cottage with the abandoned garden where Amy Fenwick lived is still owned by the people across the road from it. And they're called Wheatcroft, and you've got a member of your staff—'

'Called Joan Wheatcroft, and yes, I think that's where she was brought up . . .'

'Marion says the reason Fernley Cottage is derelict now is because the Wheatcrofts can't get the planning permission they want to do it up. They only lease the land and there's something called a superior owner . . .'

'That'll be the freeholder, and if my memory is correct all that land round the Common is now owned by Peregrine Properties.'

'Well, Marion didn't get that far. All she knew was that the Wheatcrofts can't get permission to improve Fernley Cottage because what you call the freeholder won't let them. What do these Peregrine people want it for? To build flats on it?'

'They want to do whatever will bring in the money. But I'm glad you found out about the cottage. I'll have a word about it with Joan. Take her mind off the wedding.'

Joan Wheatcroft worked for Franklyn Davey, who had just been made partner at Gillorns, and was about to marry his Dinah. The marriage would take place in Ireland and several members of the staff had been invited – including Joan, who had been told so many outrageous tales of the Irish by her boss that she considered the place far more of a foreign country than Spain, where she had been twice on holiday. 'Dinah's dad . . .' she exclaimed to her friends, '. . . he's so poor he does his rounds on a donkey cart, and him a doctor, too . . .' Not realizing that Franklyn was winding her up, she wondered if they'd be able to afford a wedding cake, or would it be that soda bread stuff they gave you for breakfast . . . And that photograph Dinah had shown her of the house . . . . It was a ruin, two stark gables and a lot of ivy! What neither of them had told Joan was that there was a lovely modern bungalow alongside; the old place was quite simply kept for the benefit of the tourists.

As it was Franklyn and Dinah's joke and no concern of his, Kemp didn't enlighten Joan either when he stopped her on the way out of the office at lunchtime.

'Where do you generally go?' he asked.

'Just round to the Dairy-Bar for a sandwich.'

'Mind if I join you?'

Surprised, but equal to it. 'Not at all, Mr Kemp. I'm on my own today. Sometimes Steve joins me, but he's working.' Steve was the current boyfriend; he might or might not stay the course.

Sitting with his elbows on the milk-white top of one of the little tables, Kemp asked if her family were still out at the Common.

'Only Grandma. Mum and Dad took the first chance they had to get on the council estate. Grandma's place is Stone Age, like it's been there for ever . . . And there's nothing she will do about it . . .'

'But you lived there, Joan, when you were little?'

'I was born there at Sycamore Cottage, and I lived there till I was about ten, I reckon. I still go out and see Grandma Wheatcroft – that's what we call her so she's not mixed up with my mum's mum.'

Kemp was trying to work out Joan's age. She had been with the firm for four years, and had come straight from secretarial college. That would make her about twenty-five.

'So you must have gone to Oldgreen Primary School?'

'I started there but then they closed it later and we all went to the one in the town, so I don't remember much about it.'

'Was the little boy Fenwick there with you?

Joan had been gurgling something soapy from the bottom of her milky tumbler. She stopped and looked up, goggle-eyed.

'Is that it, Mr Kemp? This is all about the murder?'

Kemp hadn't been prepared for her to be so direct. 'Yes,' he said, 'in a way it is. Did you know Rickie?'

Joan shook her head. 'To be perfectly honest, I can't even remember what he looked like. I would have been a rising five that summer, and Rickie was in one of the top forms, so I wouldn't have known him. But of course once it happened . . . Everybody talking about it, you couldn't help feeling you'd known him even if you hadn't . . . Do you get what I'm saying?'

'Indeed I do. It's a common enough feeling, older people get it more than children – perhaps because they've more to remember.'

Joan was shredding her straw. 'I think,' she said, slowly, 'I could remember Rickie Fenwick if I really tried . . . There was that play they put on that summer, on the Common, and we were all in it . . .' She wrinkled her nose, frowning. 'I do remember the feel of my silk fairy frock. Even us little uns got to be fairies. They say he was like an elf – Rickie, I mean. If I think very hard about it I get this sense of wonder, like magic . . . Then it all goes. Gets all sort of squashed, like . . . And what's left is a blur . . . something snatched away. Does that sound silly to you?'

'Not in the least. It sounds like the echo of a true experience. Eat your sandwiches while I think about it.'

Later, she said to him: 'Of course as I got older and we all ended up in the other school it wasn't talked about so much. Not that our parents had talked about it anyway, not when we were around.'

'But among yourselves, the other children? Do you remember being scared?'

Joan shook her head vigorously. 'We kids weren't scared exactly but we did feel that things were being kept from us.' She picked out a piece of tomato and ate it separately. 'We wondered why our dads and mums shied away from the subject as if it was dog shit on their shoes . . .' She grinned. 'Well, of course we know now to them it was dirt. Am I talking too much, Mr Kemp?'

'No. Go on. I really am interested.'

'The bigger boys in the playground, we'd hear them talking about it. They said there was something awful about Rickie's death, something really nasty. After all, to us kids death didn't mean a lot to us. We'd mebbe had someone in the family die, my mum lost a baby about that time but it didn't mean anything to me, and there was a girl in our class who died from pneumonia and we were all sorry but it wasn't real to us . . . What I'm trying to say is that it wasn't Rickie's actual death that bothered us, it was all the secret stuff they wouldn't talk about, so some of the boys were making things up, like Rickie'd been tortured . . . We'd all seen films on television about Japanese prisoner-of-war camps, so that might explain things, that Rickie's death was just too horrible to talk about. Then another boy, a real know-all, said it was to do with sex. Well, that shut everybody up, I can tell you, because sex was something nobody knew anything about because it was something only grown-ups did and was no concern of ours . . . Sex was like having to learn geography, boring, boring . . .'

She grinned broadly. 'You'd hardly believe it, would you? When we finally got to know about sex it was interesting enough but no reason for all that mystery. We could have worked it out for ourselves, and most of us did.'

'Do you remember Perce Cavendish?' asked Kemp.

Joan screwed up her forehead. 'Funny you should ask that . . . He was completely blanked out by our parents, he might never have existed. If I think hard about that hot summer – for it was hot and sunny a lot of the time, and that's not just childish memory, my dad talks about how early they had the hay in that year – I get the impression of someone tall and skinny who was always leaping about, and he had a lovely voice . . . But as far as the grown-ups were concerned he was never there at all. I remember when I was a teenager asking my mother whatever happened to the man who put on that play, and she said, 'What man? The play was put on by your school teachers.'

She jumped up from her seat. 'Look at the time, Mr Kemp, I should have been back in the office ten minutes ago. Mr Davey will go spare . . .'

'Tell Franklyn that you had an important conference with me. And thank you for talking so freely, Joan. It looks as if your innocence at the time saved you from a nastier memory.'

'Ignorance, more like,' said Joan as they left the café. 'Our parents kept us in the dark but I'm not sure it was a good idea. They should have told us the truth about Rickie's death. Oh, I know,' she went on, hurriedly, 'we'd not heard of paedophilia at the time, only not to take sweets from strangers for they would be poisoned, and not to get into cars with men we didn't know, fat chance of that where I was concerned. I lived right over from the school and there were never any cars on the Common in those days . . .' She hesitated a moment. 'If you really want to know more about the murder you should talk to my gran. She never minded talking about what happened, only Mum used to shut her up, and still does, says she's a bit wandered in the head now she's got to eighty. But I think she's very much all there. I go out on Saturday afternoons sometimes with Steve, and I get her shopping in now she can't go to the supermarket.'

'I would very much like to meet your gran, and not just to talk about Rickie Fenwick. Let me know what time you're going on Saturday and I'll drive you up there.'

Six

Some Saturdays, however, would have to pass before Kemp was able to take Joan Wheatcroft up on the promise to visit her grandmother. Other events intervened.

Only a few days after they had met at the Sutherlands' dinner party he was surprised to get a phone call from Lettice Aumary. She was businesslike, even perfunctory, but he sensed an underlying note of distress.

'We talked the other night about Roger,' she said, without preamble, 'and you know the truth of it. It would do me a kindness if you would visit him, he keeps asking for you. Even that in itself is strange, he normally hates to see people . . . particularly those whom he knew in his better years.'

'But I hardly knew Roger at all,' protested Kemp. 'We were never on any set of terms . . . Why on earth does he want to see me?

She didn't answer the question directly. 'He's really very ill. Torvil says that unless he consents to treatment, he won't last . . .'

Despite the fact that there was something like entreaty in her voice, Kemp hesitated. Did he really want to get mixed up in the troubles of an alcoholic, particularly one whose place in his memory he would have preferred to be vacant? There were certain things one could never entirely forget, and physical violence was one of them. Kemp had indeed been surprised in the days since Lettice Warrender had reappeared in his life how sharp had become that

38

memory of the encounter with her brother, and the man who was now her husband. Instinct told him to shun all present circumstance which might revive feelings which he had thought satisfactorily buried . . . But there was a shake in her voice now to which he had to respond.

'Lennox . . . please see him . . .'

'If you think it will help . . .'

An evening was agreed, and Lettice would drive: 'Roger's at his flat, where he's being looked after by a friend . . . It's on the outskirts of London – quicker if I take you. I've been trying to see him as often as I can now that we're over here, but sometimes he can be . . . difficult . . .'

'What was that all about?' asked Mary, who knew that it had been Lettice on the line. When he told her, she was curious. 'Why should he want to see you? Perhaps it's to apologize for beating you up.'

'And that's been long forgiven and forgotten,' said her husband, untruthfully. He had become uneasy in his mind about anything to do with Lettice and her family as if the subject was brittle and might fall apart if dwelt on.

Being driven by her in the direction of London a few evenings later, Kemp found his troubled thoughts were not helped by the fact that the hired car was of a top-notch breed with which she was obviously not familiar. 'I tend to leave such things to Tod,' she almost apologized. 'I'd have been perfectly happy with a Mini . . .'

Talking motor cars was not one of Kemp's favourite things but he did ask politely what she drove in the States. Apparently, since they lived in New York, she didn't have a car of her own but simply hired when wanted. 'That must be why you're a bit out of practice,' he observed. 'The sign back there said forty miles an hour, you're doing a good sixty . . .'

Lettice braked sharply, and swore under her breath. 'I'm just not used to this sort of car . . .'

To keep it friendly, Kemp asked about Torvil's lecture tour. He was up in Edinburgh for a few days at a medical conference. 'He's very much in demand,' said Lettice, 'since he pioneered a new line in diabetic treatment. That's why we'll be at least six weeks over here.'

'And you? Are you pleased to be back, visiting old haunts and looking up old friends?'

'Well, no, I haven't, actually . . . The mere thought of Castleton House as a kind of peoples' palace doesn't exactly thrill me.'

'It's a business park, not an outdoor circus . . . There's a boating lake and a golf course. I thought you'd approve. You were once in favour of the Development Corporation's ideals . . .'

'That was a long time ago, and I was young.' Lettice evidently wanted to shrug off her former self. Kemp felt like telling this stuffy American matron to get down off her high horse but it might be impolite to tell her so. He decided to remain silent.

Perhaps aware that she was not being companionable, Lettice told him that her main concern of the moment was Roger. Since he had been out of the rehab centre they had managed to arrange for him to have a housekeeper at his flat. She stammered over the words 'to look after him', so that Kemp got the impression of a watchful dragon, but one who could also cook and dust the furniture.

This is not going to be an outing of much joy, he told himself, gloomily. It didn't help that they were now caught in a traffic jam outside Leatown, a place he had been avoiding for years, not because of its twisted streets and crazy one-way system but because of the bad memories it held for him.

It was in this old town, squeezed between the River Lea and the Forest, that he had had his first practice, lived with Muriel, planned a cloudless future and thought himself settled for life. Disaster and its consequences had crept up slowly, toying carelessly with their lives before striking them down. Muriel's little penchant for gambling seemed trivial at first until the addiction got out of hand and ugly. The bills got paid somehow until there was nothing left, yet the gambling went on and the threats grew more real, more physical, until the last, the acid that would be thrown . . . Muriel of the fine-spun hair and the porcelain skin . . . Muriel at his feet in despair . . . the botched suicide attempt . . . And there the money lay, snug and easy in its trust fund, not likely to be accounted for in years, the money that would save her . . .

Kemp was aware that Lettice was apologizing for the hold-up as if it was her fault. He tried to clear his mind of the thoughts that bubbled to the surface unbidden as the car edged forward through familiar streets. 'I never come this way,' he said, without thinking. 'I usually take the Epping Road.'

'I'm only taking this route because it brings us out nearer to where Roger has his flat. I don't blame you for hating Leatown after what happened to you there.' Lettice's tone was flat; she might well have been talking about traffic.

Kemp was aghast. How could she possibly have known what he was feeling? But, of course, he'd told her, twenty years ago. There had been no one more sympathetic than Lettice Warrender, no one else to whom he could talk so freely. She had been quick to understand why he hadn't hesitated to embezzle that money, and she had taken full measure of the subsequent calamity, the sudden death of a beneficiary, and the inevitable scrutiny of the fund. Struck off by the Law Society, he had only escaped criminal prosecution by the clemency of the clients and his commitment to them that every penny would be repaid . . .

'I'd forgotten,' he said, now, recognizing that he was not telling the truth; Lettice deserved better from him. 'Well, perhaps it would be more honest to admit that I prefer not to think about it any more. So much has happened since . . . you know Muriel died in, of all places, Las Vegas? She followed her casino-owner all the way out there, and married him. When he died he left her the whole of his gambling empire. Ironic, don't you think?'

'Americans haven't got a highly developed sense of irony.' Lettice found an opening between two lorries, and spurred the car into it. In a little while they had a clear road, and Kemp relaxed; back there he'd wondered if they would make it. Lettice's driving was as erratic as the shifts in her conversation.

'When I got to know you first,' she was saying, 'I thought you were the most honest person I'd ever met. You made everyone else look like the phonies they were, and when you told me why you'd had to stop being a lawyer and you'd become an enquiry agent – you wouldn't even call yourself a detective – I thought of you as a hero.'

The interior of a car at night can be one of the most intimate places. Conversations that cannot bear the light of day, confessions and revelations too deeply felt, opinions too firmly held, all these can be loosened and made more easy by the darkness only lit by the spasmodic flashes from motorway lights and the long bland stretches of shop windows. Here, sealed in this small capsule, faces are blurred and give-away eyes and mouths cannot be seen.

When Lettice said the words 'I thought of you as a hero', Kemp felt his heart lurch. So, that was what it had been, hero-worship . . . He should have known at the time but he'd been too wrapped up in his own preliminary troubles getting back into law to recognize something so very obvious in his relationship with the young girl.

'I heard them talking about you at home,' Lettice went on, 'the new solicitor at Gillorns. Mother had always dealt with Mr Archie up at Clement's Inn. She thought the

Newtown practice suburban and nasty, so what did they expect but a lawyer who'd been struck off?'

Kemp felt like protesting that he'd been reinstated by then. It was so much like living in an old story . . .

'And then you told me all about it, very matter-of-fact you were, in the Cabbage White pub at lunchtime. You'd rescued me from those terrible grey filing cabinets and the gawping old women that went with them . . . You were like something out of a book to me, you were the wronged man but also the man who would put things right – the Philip Marlowe of Newtown . . .'

Young Lettice had always had a great turn of phrase; Kemp sensed that it hadn't been used in years. Somehow it didn't fit in with the image of her in America. He was desperately trying to put together the real present-day Lettice Aumary who kept on giving out contradictory messages; at the Sutherlands she had appeared the typical well-to-do American woman, secure in her position as the wife of a respected man, yet even then there had been an unexpected outburst, like the petulant stamp of a girl, over who among them had known Perce Cavendish. And what was Kemp to make of this other Lettice, his companion tonight, who was telling him things he didn't actually want to know? Hero-worship, indeed . . . He was left almost speechless, but had to respond in some way.

'I'm sorry,' he said, lamely, 'I never realized you had seen me as a character out of fiction. At the time I felt more like a fish out of water . . . It took quite an effort to climb out. What I do remember is your sympathy, how you listened to me . . .' His words seemed inadequate in view of what she had been saying, but he could not find better ones.

She was laughing. 'Don't worry, Lennox, I don't have heroes any more. I've grown up. Now, do you know this part of Wanstead? We're nearly there. Roger lives in Crownberry Avenue.'

'Yes, I do know it. They were the houses of Victorian merchants making their money in the East End but keeping their wives and daughters in the green lands well away from the smoke. The properties took a dip in fortunes after the War but I hear they've recovered.'

'Very much so. Roger has a lovely flat . . .'

Conversation seemed to have returned to the ordinary.

'Is he still working?' he asked. He was going to meet someone who was almost a stranger; he had to have some term of reference.

'I think he's too ill at present. He's in a firm in the City but we don't know much about it.' She sounded irritated. 'It's years since I saw Roger – it was a shock, his appearance, I mean. I ought to warn you, he looks nothing like he used to . . .'

As Kemp had only a vague memory of Roger Warrender's looks he assured her he would not be shocked – he'd met alcoholics before, in or out of rehabilitation centres. The one mentioned by Torvil and Lettice was expensive, but only the best would have been good enough for the Warrender family, no matter their straitened circumstances. He'd liked to have asked Lettice outright as to whether Roger had that kind of money but thought it better to walk the proverbial eggshells with her lest he get thrown out of the car. Instead he considered how the windfall they must have received from the Newtown Development Corporation might have been dispersed.

Roger was the son and heir: that would matter to Lionel and Paula under the old laws of inheritance, quite apart from the fact that they tended to regard Lettice as an errant twig on the family tree. Anyway, she'd married her cousin who was doing nicely so she wouldn't be short of a bob or two.

As if she had reached into his mind, she broke in: 'It's just as well the flat's big enough to take most of the

Castleton House stuff. Roger was always more attached to it anyway than I was. He likes to have reminders of our old life around him.'

A sentimental drinker, even if temporarily on the wagon, wasn't going to be much of a host. Kemp enquired about the housekeeper.

'She's Millicent Maitland. And – you'll laugh at this, Lennox – she's the niece of the last nanny we had as children at Castleton. She qualified as a nurse but most of her work is private. She's so good with Roger . . . We're lucky to have found her.'

The car turned into a short driveway between bushes. 'We've arrived,' she said. 'It's the ground-floor flat.'

Seven

The house must have been a substantial mansion in former days and even now still had an air of wealth and luxurious living. Lettice shivered a little on getting out of the car for the night wind was cold. They stood for a moment in the stone portico after she pulled the bell chain. A hanging lamp in red and blue stained glass hung above the door, and swayed in the uprush of air from the garden, so that Kemp's first impression of Millicent Maitland was indeed of a dragon's face, one bathed in blood. Only when she stepped back to let them in did the crimson tide ebb to show her as a normal person, sharp featured but smiling.

'Good evening, Lettice,' she said, 'it's a cold night out there . . .' She had a level voice, friendly and without accent. She may have been a paid employee but she was standing no nonsense. She watched Lettice put her coat on the hall stand but she turned to take Kemp's. 'I'm glad that Mr Roger is having visitors, he needs people to talk to . . .'

'How has he been?' Lettice spoke in the hushed tone of one in a hospital corridor.

'Better, I think, but restless. He's had something on his mind, he says, and that's why he asked you to bring Mr Kemp.'

'Oh, sorry!' Lettice was acting like a hostess who's forgotten to put out the sherry. 'This is Lennox Kemp. We've known each other a long time, and he used to know Roger, too. Lennox, this is Millicent Maitland.'

The hall carpet was soft and deep, and their footfalls made no sound on it. Indeed the whole atmosphere in the flat was one of hushed calm where to raise one's voice would be like an intrusion on some private grief. When Miss Maitland opened the sitting-room door Kemp saw at once what Lettice had meant about Roger's attachment to the place of his childhood. For they were all here: the greens and golds of the Castleton furnishings, the gleaming mahogany bureau, the two walnut credenzas that had stood at either end of the vast drawing room now standing side by side along one wall as if to defend their right never to be separated, glass wall cabinets stuffed with china, the walls themselves in Georgian green covered thickly with the family portraits, the darkly blurred oil paintings and faint watercolours, and all the mishmash of stuff wealthy Victorian travellers had plundered from Greece or Italy as they made their Grand Tours unhampered by modern conscience . . .

The room was big, but unfortunately not big enough; the effect was of a small museum overwhelmed by the generosity of a donor they couldn't refuse . . .

'Mr Roger will be in presently,' said Miss Maitland, arranging chairs for them, 'and then I'll bring some tea.' She turned to Kemp. 'I'm sorry, Mr Kemp, we do not have drinks in the house. I'm sure you understand.'

Kemp understood very well – though he could have done with a stiff whisky to get him through the evening ahead. There was a shuffling sound at the door, which was pushed wide open as Roger Warrender came through it. He advanced, smiling, as if before an audience expectant on some kind of appearance. 'Hullo, Letty, nice of you to come.' He turned the same smile on Kemp. 'I see you've brought Mr Kemp. Well, old boy, still solving murders, eh?'

That little charade over, Roger sat down in the largest of the armchairs, brought up behind him unobstrusively by the housekeeper, who then effaced herself, murmuring something about tea. When the door closed behind her Roger sighed, a stage effect meant to be interpreted as lighthearted, and there was a short silence.

It was over twenty years since Kemp had seen Lettice's brother. Then Roger would have been about twenty-three, a tall good-looking youth if a little petulant about the mouth, and with arrogance in his eyes, which were like his mother's. Now only the voice, the high-pitched public school accent, remained. The face was cavernous, the whole body shrunk, so that Kemp could scarcely recognize it as belonging to the same person. Words sprang to his mind, words out of textbooks on feudal law – the doctrine of waste. Roger Warrender was a wasted asset. Physical ruin in the lank hair, grey-streaked, the yellow-white skin, the blackened teeth and the skeletal limbs incapable of filling out the expensive suit, but even worse was the hopelessness, the slack features and the deadness of expression in a face pulled down by gravity and unable to raise itself.

Lettice was making banal conversation, touching gingerly on medical matters as if reassuring herself something was being done about this wreck of a brother, and Kemp's heart went out to her. He himself had assumed the false, hearty manner he disparaged in other people's attitude to invalids; he couldn't help himself. Eventually he found they were talking about Newtown, and he answered Roger's original joking comment by saying he was now much too busy earning an honest living to have any spare time for solving murders. He talked about his office, and acknowledged it had grown from what Roger was describing as a 'poky little hole on the town square' but he soon became aware that, like most alcoholics, Roger's only interest was in himself.

To Kemp the whole scene was artificial as if it was taking place in a film he had seen, or a book he had read. Fishing about in his mind while he kept up this meaningless conversation with Roger – to which Lettice had become a mere onlooker as if afraid to break something – he found what he'd been looking for. It was a book, it was from Anthony Powell's *Dance to the Music of Time*. Roger was Charles Stringham and, surely, Miss Maitland was playing the part of Tuffy Weedon, who had been deputized by his family, as it were, to look after him . . . Kemp had been so caught up with his half memory of the book, and his knowledge that it was not unusual for families to treat any of their kin who had become alcoholic or drug-addicted as if they were victims of some unmentionable disease and held at arm's length, that he had missed part of what was being said.

Lettice was telling her brother about the Sutherlands' dinner party, and for some reason the subject had angered Roger. He turned on her and raised his voice.

'Oh, for God's sake, Letty, you've told me all that before. That's why I asked you to bring Kemp . . . Sorry, old boy, quite forgot . . . Things aren't always what they seem . . .' He moved restlessly in the big chair. 'Where the devil's that woman got to? I need a drink . . .' Then with mock seriousness to Lettice: 'Don't get your knickers in a twist, my dear, I hear what the medicos say . . . I only want tea . . . Oh, God, I feel terrible . . .'

He suddenly looked drained; sweat stood out on his forehead. Lettice looked on, helplessly, then she got up abruptly. 'I'll go and get Millicent,' she said, and whisked smartly out of the door.

'Those damned pills,' said Roger, 'they only last for a while. You ever been on pills, Kemp? Then don't let them get you started . . .'

'What did you think of your time at The Priory?' Kemp asked, trying to get some footing for talk with the man.

'Waste of bloody money . . . They've got 'em all over the place, you know. Not just one Priory but hundreds . . . It's

49

a conspiracy, old chap, that's what it is . . .' He stopped, his brow furrowed with an effort of thought. 'There was something I had to tell you . . . Blessed if I can remember . . . That's what happens when they give you pills, you don't remember things you want to . . .' His voice trailed off.

Quite suddenly he was pushing himself to his feet. 'Got to have a pee, old man. Be back shortly . . .'

It was a sad shuffle he made towards a door at the far end of the room, the carpet slippers on his slow feet making him all the more like an old man. Although he was tempted to do so, Kemp felt it would be an unwise move to take his arm. Roger turned at the door after pulling it open. 'Don't go away. Something to tell you . . . memory isn't what it was. I wanted to say I was sorry . . . you know, about what happened . . .' He was clinging on to the door as if for support, then he was through it, and gone.

Kemp waited. It wasn't much of an apology perhaps but after all these years he'd never really expected one. Somewhere in Roger's muddled head the need to say something must have lurked, and presumably Lettice's mention of Kemp being at the recent dinner party had brought it out. Well, if that was all there was to be this evening then Kemp was ready to go home.

However, he must attend his host's return, and as if to emphasize that some hospitality was involved, Lettice and Miss Maitland came in, the housekeeper pushing a laden trolley. There was a large tea urn, hot sausage rolls, a variety of sandwiches and a chocolate sponge. Not exactly what one would call an evening meal, thought Kemp, but in this kind of household perhaps there was a looseness about the timing for afternoon tea.

Lettice was looking at Roger's empty chair as if apprehending unwelcome news. 'He's just gone to the loo,' Kemp explained, lest she blame him for spiriting her brother away. He wondered if Millicent held all the house keys and

Roger's wallet as well, otherwise what would stop him legging it to the nearest pub?

'Has he been talking to you, Lennox?' Lettice enquired, anxiously.

'Of course,' said Kemp, stating the obvious; they would hardly have been sitting in silence. Not that they'd had much conversation, and none of it, save perhaps Roger's stammering words at the door, very productive. 'I think Roger is having trouble with his memory,' he said, diplomatically. It was Millicent who nodded her assent.

'Mr Roger does keep forgetting things, and it worries him,' she said as she poured out. 'Sugar, Mr Kemp?' He shook his head. He wanted to say that perhaps Roger Warrender ought to get out more but it seemed too flippant a remark in the circumstances. 'What do the doctors think of Roger's condition?' he asked.

Again it was Millicent who answered as Lettice hesitated. 'They say he's making progress,' she said, primly. 'His attitude is more positive than it was.'

That sounded to Kemp more like psychological jargon than sound medical opinion but it perked Lettice up no end so that she exclaimed: 'Oh, I'm so glad. I do hate it when he's depressed.'

Kemp bit into a sausage roll. The pastry was light and flaky, the centre delicious. 'But I thought you hadn't seen him in years. How long has he been suffering from depression?'

'It's not manic or anything as bad as that,' she hastened to assure him. 'I may not have seen much of Roger, of course, but Torvil is over here a lot and he's been keeping an eye on him. And we were so lucky to find Millie, she does wonders.' By now Lettice was positively gushing. Well, if Millie's wardship was as good as her baking, they had indeed got themselves a treasure.

'Dr Aumary had heard of me through a medical

colleague,' said Miss Maitland, smoothly, 'and naturally when I heard it was Mr Roger they were concerned about, well, I didn't hesitate.' Despite her quiet, small voice she gave the impression that not only was she top of the class in caring but also the Warrenders were fortunate in finding her. Kemp wasn't sure which attitude he found the more nauseating. On the other hand she certainly knew a thing or two about catering, and when the plate was offered he indulged himself again with a couple of smoked salmon sandwiches.

A noise at the far door signalled the return of their host. This time his step seemed more sure and the ghastly Terry Thomas grin more prominent as he weaved his way through the furniture towards his chair. No sooner had he sat down than he reached out for the trolley.

'Ain't she marvellous, our Millie?' There was a mocking glint in his eye as he helped himself to a sausage roll with a hand that only slightly shook. Silently, Millicent gave him a plate and a paper napkin; it seemed to symbolize their relationship.

'Wanted to ask you something, Kemp . . .' Roger said, between mouthfuls. 'You don't mind if I call you Kemp. It's how we always thought of you . . .'

'I'd rather have Lennox if these are the terms we're on. I've never called you Warrender, have I? It's unlikely we shared the same public school.'

'A hit, a hit, a very palpable hit . . .' Roger's guffaw ended in a fit of coughing. 'That was the other thing about you,' he spluttered. 'You were too smart with words.'

'A lawyer would be at a loss without them,' said Kemp, lightly. He was determined not to take offence. 'But you said you had something you wanted to ask me, Roger?'

'Did I? Can't for the life of me remember what it was.' He took, without thanks, the slice of sponge cake handed to him by Millicent, and turned to his sister. 'What's old

Torvil driving these days, Letty? He used to like them sleek and powerful. Your car's the impression you want to give of yourself, he used to say.'

'He's hired a Mercedes. He doesn't get much opportunity to drive at home. Anyway, those ideas of his, they were only the idle conceits of youth . . .'

'Oh, lah di dah . . . Don't tell me that red Ferrari he got on graduation was only an idle conceit . . .' Roger was mocking her. Then he fell silent, brooding. Old resentments run deep, thought Kemp, watching him, but they rise to the surface when the waters are troubled. It had happened to him recently and now it seemed that Roger was sharing the same current. 'All I got was your old Morris Minor and Dad's promise that things would be better next year. They didn't bloody well get better, did they, not that year or ever?' He sank further into his chair, staring ahead, seeing nothing except some personal vision of a time long ago when there might have been hope.

Eventually he roused himself as if the silence which he had made round the trolley had become unbearable. 'What d'you call them, Letty? Youthful conceits? D'you mean schoolboy pranks, is that it? You don't know the half of it, Sis . . . Does she, Lennox Kemp?'

If he was referring to what Kemp thought he was referring to, then he agreed. Had Lettice Warrender known, either at the time or later, that Torvil Aumary and Roger Warrender had taken it into their heads to teach Kemp a lesson? It was a question he had preferred not to think about but, looking at her now and seeing her at once puzzled and no more than irritated by her brother, he was pretty certain she had never known.

'Oh, you and Torvil were always up to something in those days, but at least he had the sense to grow up . . .'

Roger didn't seem to be listening. He was regarding Kemp with what could only be described as a beady eye.

Behind it Kemp got the impression of rusty machinery cranking up as if to make up for lost time . . .

Again, he prompted, gently. 'You had something to ask of me, Roger?'

Since he had absented himself – if only for that short time – Roger seemed more voluble, even brighter, despite the petulant descent into memories of unhappy youth. Drumming fingers on the edge of his chair, he was about to speak when Miss Maitland roused herself into her hostess role and announced that she must clear away the supper things.

Lettice hurried to help her. 'Of course,' she said, 'we've already taken up enough of your time.'

'And what about my time, doesn't that count any more?' Roger shouted after them as they gathered up the dishes, piled them on the trolley, and went out to the kitchen. 'Bloody women . . .' The clatter they had made seemed to annoy him, and he pushed his hands up over his ears and into his hair.

He looked so like a fugitive that Kemp felt a sudden pity for him. 'Is there anything I can do to help you, Roger?' he said, and meant it.

Roger drew his fingers roughly down his face, which was drawn and tired.

'Just come and see me again,' he said, simply. 'Look, I'll give you my phone number . . .' He struggled to his feet, caught his toe on the chair leg and stumbled. The noise brought Lettice rushing in from the kitchen. He stood, swaying, and stared at her. 'It's all right, Sis . . . I can walk on my own. Why don't you mind your own bloody business and I'll mind mine?'

Lettice turned red. 'Just don't call me Sis,' she said.

Roger laughed. 'You never did like it, did you? Torvil and me winding up the old Pater and Mater . . . talking like those yoicks on the council estates. Blokes like the Rodings,

54

not a brain between them, in and out of jail like a couple of yo-yos . . Came from what Ma used to call the low streets . . . Not 'arf, they did . . .'

By the time Roger had finished this little harangue he was scrabbling about in the desk top. Lettice went to help him but he pushed her away, not too gently.

Kemp was beginning to lose what sympathy he'd had for her brother. The Rodings had been clients of his, not a bad family but disadvantaged in ways never recognized by people like the Warrenders. However, he held his peace and rose to his feet. As far as he was concerned, the evening was over.

He had come as near to liking Roger as he was ever going to but the man's boorish behaviour towards his sister stopped even that tolerance.

Later, he would ask himself why he had asked the question. Out of pique because Roger must have known Kemp had twice defended the Roding brothers in court, out of a desire to get his own back for slights earlier in the evening, or simple anger at remembered injury?

'By the way, Roger, did you know Perce Cavendish?'

Still at the desk, Warrender had his back to him. There was a moment of hesitation before he turned and stared at Kemp. 'Well, well,' he said, softly, 'now there's a coincidence . . . Perce Cavendish? How could anyone ever have known Perce Cavendish? He was the man who never was . . . Funny, you should ask . . .'

He began to walk, quite briskly for him, back to his chair, shrugging off Lettice's tentative offer of help. Once settled, he raised an eyebrow at Kemp as if expecting more questions, but just at that moment Millie Maitland bustled in with coats for the guests. 'It's colder than ever out there,' she said, making an unnecessary fuss. 'You must wrap up warm.'

Roger muttered something under his breath. He held out

the scrap of paper he'd been writing on at the bureau. 'That's my telephone number, if you can bear to come again to see the old inebriate . . .'

Now, when Kemp would have liked to have stayed longer, both ladies were in a flurry to put an end to the visit. He thrust the note into his pocket, and his arms into the sleeves of the coat which Millie was already slipping expertly over his shoulders. She could have been butler also in this household where she had so many duties. Kemp wondered if, when he and Lettice had gone, Millie would put Roger to bed . . . The niece of an old nanny at Castleton, Lettice had said. Well, the call to nursemaid members of the Warrender clan might run in the Maitland genes . . .

Eight

Lennox Kemp took the crumpled piece of paper from his pocket and smoothed it out on the table beside his large brandy glass. Mary had laughed at his immediate request on returning home. 'I've never seen a man so in need of a drink,' she said when he had explained, but Kemp had been glad of it. The drive home with Lettice had been in almost complete silence, both probably worried by the same problem but too embarrassed to speak of it; Roger lay in their minds like a left-over leaf in autumn, a piece of unfinished business but out of their scope.

'What do you really think of Roger?' Lettice had asked him, her face momentarily visible in a blinking traffic light. She looked both stern and sad. It was a question which required the truth but Kemp was reluctant to give her the whole of it. It was clear to him that it wasn't just a craving for alcohol that was wasting Roger Warrender; white powders of whatever kind are easier to stash away than hefty bottles of booze, and certainly something had sparked Roger up on his visit to the lavatory. How long he had been a drug addict and whether his stimulant was heroin or cocaine was irrelevant to anyone not immediately concerned with the medical problem. What worried Kemp was whether Lettice knew. Her husband must have recognized the symptoms but Kemp had no idea how often Torvil had been seeing his brother-in-law over recent years. Presumably the two attempts at rehabilitation were the result of some kind of consultation, and Kemp remembered that the Sutherlands had both known of Roger's condition and must have guessed how serious it was, which explained their unwillingness to gossip.

Kemp himself had faltered in trying to give Lettice a proper answer.

'I think he's quite seriously ill,' he had said, in the car, thankful that she could not see his face. Lettice had always been one of those people to whom the expression 'looked you straight in the eye' meant just that. 'Perhaps another stay at this Priory place might do him good . . .' At least they would be familiar with drug addiction and its consequences if untreated. 'I don't think it's altogether right for him to be alone in that flat – despite the wonderful Miss Maitland.' To anyone else he might have said, flippantly, that Roger should get out more, but this did not seem the right occasion.

Lettice said nothing for a few miles; she didn't even comment on his passing swipe at her friend, Miss Maitland. But when she did speak it was obvious that things had been boiling up inside her.

'I can't think why you asked him about Perce Cavendish. As if Roger doesn't have worries enough of his own. Why should you bring up something about a man who's long dead?'

Kemp remained silent as Lettice used the gears in a way the car resented. When it recovered and was running more or less smoothly she returned to the subject as to a nagging tooth. This time she sounded more angry than simply irritated.

'Just because you've got an obsession about this old case, Lennox, I don't know why you need to bother Roger with it. Of course he knew Cavendish – he and Torvil used to make fun of him . . . He was a bit of a nuisance, a hanger-on, you know . . . And of course nobody knew the truth till afterwards . . .'

In the same way in which she was handling the car, all this was coming out jerkily as though she was gathering up past thoughts at random. Kemp let her run on.

She appeared to have every intention of doing so. 'We want Roger to be thinking positively,' she said. 'That's the way forward for him. The last thing we want is for him to get morbid. It's not good for him to be looking back – and yet that's exactly what you were doing asking him about that man. I would have thought that you of all people would have been more understanding of Roger's need at the moment to get himself a future rather than rake up the past.'

Kemp wasn't sure whether Lettice was referring to his own situation when he had first come to Newtown, and he thought she wasn't sure either, she was beset by the problem of Roger, of course, and uncertain how to deal with it – even in conversation. All he could do was murmur that of course he understood, and she was quite right. He felt he had been reproved by a rather uptight but sympathetic head-mistress.

He told his wife now that, although still on superficial speaking terms, by the time Lettice dropped him off at home their special relationship had dwindled somewhat. Mary had listened, and only commented that he should have at least brought Lettice in for coffee before her drive back to London. Kemp said he had indeed asked her but she had refused on the grounds that Torvil was due back the following day and they wanted to have some time together before he had to go back to Edinburgh next week – presumably to glean whatever harvest he expected from seeds sown at his first meeting with his professional colleagues in the North. When Lettice spoke of her husband's work she tended to do so in tones of some reverence, which Kemp found contagious. What she was actually saying was that she wanted to get to bed early, her evening with Roger being particularly stressful. As Kemp watched her drive off he was conscious that there were a lot of jagged edges in both her manner of speaking and behaviour but there was nothing he could do to smooth them out.

Looking down at the piece of paper with Roger Warrender's telephone number, Mary exclaimed: 'But look what he's written underneath!'

Kemp hadn't noticed. The figures were clear enough but below them the marks were faint as if a ballpoint was running dry. Now he could make out the words: 'Come alone.'

'Well, well, so he doesn't even want sister there.' He couldn't remember whether there had been time for Roger to scribble the words after Kemp had asked him that question about Perce Cavendish which had so bothered Lettice ... But whatever the mystery, it would have to wait, and Mary agreed with him.

'You have a business to attend to, darling, and there's the wedding next weekend. I don't think these Warrenders merit any more of your precious time.'

She was right, of course, as she generally was. His office at the moment was more than normally busy, the partners, himself included, clearing the decks before taking off for Ireland, where young Franklyn and his Dinah were to be spliced at her home on the Dingle.

'I know,' Mary went on, 'your curiosity has been roused, and that's a beast that won't lie down, but just let it alone for now.'

Kemp folded the scrap of paper and put it in his pocket. He grinned at his wife. 'How well you know me ...' He wasn't altogether sure whether that was a good thing or not.

Nine

Lennox Kemp had fully intended to comply with the wishes of his spouse and his own better self but circumstances operated against them both. On the following Friday he gave in to a sudden impulse, regardless of the fact that in the past sudden impulses had led him only to grief, and this was to be no exception.

An afternoon in Chancery on a mild case already almost over, the unfortunate indisposition of a judge which brought the proceedings to a halt meant that Kemp and his Counsel were left as it were in midair. 'Had I but known,' sighed Jeremy Young once they'd returned to his chambers, 'I could have been at my villa in Portugal.'

'And I,' said Kemp, 'could have had an extra day in Ireland.'

As it was there was nothing for it but to drive back to Newtown, and perhaps put in another hour or two at the office. He decided to go by Leatown – since the drive through the place that evening with Lettice, he had been determined to rid himself once and for all of whatever demons it held.

It was just after three when he was in Wanstead, and passing the end of Crownberry Avenue. He drew into the kerb and fished in his pocket for the piece of paper with Roger Warrender's number. He sat for a while, thinking it over. There was no reason why he should not call – Roger obviously wanted to see him, and there was really no need to let anyone else know. He used his mobile phone to call the number. The ringing tone went on for some time without any response. Then there was a tentative, shaky repeat of the number. Kemp thought he recognized the faint voice of Millicent Maitland.

'Miss Maitland? It's Lennox Kemp here. I am in the vicinity and thought I might call on Mr Warrender – if it was convenient . . .'

There was a long pause. 'Who did you say? Mr Kemp? Yes, I remember you called with Mrs Aumary . . . Can I call you back? It'll only be a few minutes.'

She sounded flustered but whether at his call or something going on in the flat it was difficult to tell. Kemp told her again that he just happened to be passing and if Mr Warrender was there he might call, again stressing whether or not it was convenient, and, yes, he would wait. He gave her the number of his mobile, and sat back, watching a sudden shower of rain batter the windscreen.

Five minutes went by, then another three. Kemp waited. I'll give her ten minutes, he thought, time to get Roger out of his bath, or dressed and in a fit state of mind. He'd really no idea whether she would call or not.

So it was almost a surprise when his mobile trilled.

'Er. Miss Maitland here. You phoned a little while ago. Are you not far away?'

She sounded distraught, a slight stammer in her voice. Kemp assured her that he was indeed close to the flat. 'I won't stay long if it's inconvenient, Miss Maitland, but Mr Warrender did ask me to come to see him again.'

'I know . . .' There was a pause. 'Well, as you are near you might as well come. I'll tell you when I see you.'

She rang off as he was thinking that was a strange thing to say.

He started up the engine, and swung the car into Crownberry Avenue, peering through the cataract that swept his windscreen until he saw the open drive between the laurel bushes. He decided to leave the car in the roadway rather than drive it up to the doorway, but as soon as he had stepped out and locked the door he regretted that decision. The sudden downpour showed no sign of stopping, and he had neither hat nor umbrella in the car. Too late to go back and restart the engine, all he could do was pull up the collar of his overcoat as he set off up the drive.

The coloured lamp was not lit in the porch, and the whole place looked grey and gloomy but at least he had shelter as he pulled on the old-fashioned bell chain.

She must have been just behind the door for it opened instantly.

'Oh, Mr Kemp . . .' she said, blinking at him as if trying to focus properly, 'I am so sorry . . .'

At first he did not think she was going to let him in. She kept apologizing for something she was finding it hard to get her tongue round. Suddenly she seemed to see his state, and she gasped.

'But you're soaking wet . . . Come in out of the rain. I'll explain in a minute, but do come in.'

Kemp became aware that raindrops were actually gushing from his coat-tails as he stepped over the threshold. He found himself apologizing as little runnels of water splashed on to the thick carpet as he stood on the spot where, on his last visit, Miss Maitland had taken his coat. She was not going to do it this time, and not because it was soaking wet. He was beginning to understand what she was trying to tell him.

Mr Roger was not receiving any visitors. Mr Roger had had a terrible night and she'd had to call the doctor in the morning. 'That's the local man who's looking after him.' He had called later and given the patient an injection to calm him down. Thankfully, Mr Roger was now asleep, and it would be unwise for him to be disturbed.

'I wouldn't dream of doing so, Miss Maitland. Of course I quite understand, and thank you for seeing me.' Kemp was finding her disjointed speech infectious and he seemed to be adopting it. 'And for explaining. I only called on the off-chance, unexpectedly passing this way from the City.'

'Well, it was difficult to tell you on the phone, Mr Kemp. It's the kind of news better given face to face, don't you think? I have let Dr Aumary and Lettice know. They will be here as soon as they can. Mr Roger's own practitioner has spoken of alcoholic damage to the liver. I think you already are aware of the seriousness of Mr Roger's illness?'

'I am indeed.' Kemp had just caught sight of himself in the long hall mirror and was immediately struck by the image of a scarecrow in a bedraggled coat, what hair he possessed plastered down above a white countenance, the forehead glistening with beaded raindrops. As he raised an arm to wipe them off, the apparition in the glass moved like a wounded bat. If such a creature had arrived at his own door he doubted whether he would have been admitted, never mind given house room. As he retreated towards the still open front door he found himself apologizing once more for his presence. 'I am so sorry to have disturbed you, Miss Maitland. You must have things to do. Please tell Mr Warrender . . . another time.'

As he reached the door, however, a gust of cold, wet air sent his coat-tails billowing around him, reminding him that he had another need.

'I'm so sorry to have to ask you . . . I left London in rather a hurry, and didn't expect this awful rain. Would you mind if I used your loo?'

As Kemp had become the more distracted, Miss Maitland herself seemed to have gained in composure. She met his request with more equanimity than she'd shown throughout his brief visit, and insisted on a detailed exposition of the bathroom situation in the flat before showing him into the drawing room and indicating the far door, from which Roger, on Kemp's previous visit, had emerged, refreshed.

When he returned to the hall she showed him out with an almost motherly admonition to get home fast, and into dry clothes before he caught cold.

Ten

The Irish wedding was a triumph for rural virtues and, as Mary Kemp observed, a slap in the face for those who believe that organization is the secret of success. She and Lennox had recently attended the wedding of a colleague's offspring where the colour of the ribbons on the bride's bouquet matched the bows on the bon-bon dishes and the tissues in the ladies' loo. The marriage of Franklyn Davey to Dinah Prescott in the small town where her father had his medical practice was disorganized to the extent of falling apart but somehow the seams held and the whole patchwork drew together to provide blessed warmth and covering for everyone who was there.

'Even Elspeth has been affected,' said Mary, on the plane back home. 'Teething troubles the week before but once in Ireland she's all smiles and chortles, basking in the lime-light.' She looked down at the sleeping child. 'For myself, Lennox, I found the whole thing hilarious but it touched the heart. When that elderly patient of Dr Prescott's got up and sang "She Moved Through the Fair" I could've wept – and me without a sentimental bone in my body.'

'Hmm . . . But there was a good dram or two of Irish whiskey in there, that brings out the sentiment in all of us.'

Kemp, too, had delighted in the wedding. He was pleased with his young colleague, Franklyn, and had just made him a partner in the firm. It was good that he had had the sense to marry his Dinah; they'd been living together for years, in the modern way, but the commitment to the stronger bond showed gravitas, a quality often called upon in his profession.

The service had also been uplifting and had touched both the Kemps in a way neither of them could put into words. Mary quietly gave thanks for her own happy marriage; out of a life of disorder and deprivation she had been blessed with a man who loved her and a child she adored. Kemp had simply looked around him and seen good people who prayed; whatever frailties they had, whatever crimes they'd committed, whatever petty betrayals and family quarrels lay behind them, for the moment they were under the protection of a benevolence greater than the ordinary world could show them.

The Kemps had stayed over the Sunday at the insistence of Dr and Mrs Prescott so that they might enjoy the calm after the storm, recover from the frolicking which had lasted into the early hours, and enjoy the benison of soft, warm Irish rain as they walked the shingle beach below the house. It was with real regret that, on the Monday morning, they had to leave both the country and the experience there, which would later be recollected in moments of tranquillity . . .

Not that, for the present, there were going to be many of these. After picking up their car at the airport, snatching a bite of lunch, and driving back to Newtown, Kemp said he'd better look in on the office to make sure nothing cataclysmic had happened to it in the absence of the senior partner. Mary assured him this was unlikely. The other members of the firm who had been at the wedding had returned on Sunday, and would have picked up the threads on Monday morning to keep the wheels rolling, she told him. He replied that she was mixing her metaphors horribly and all he wanted was to check his emails.

Strangely, it was Mary who was the first to hear the voice of Lettice Aumary.

She had fed Elspeth and put her down in her cot, still rosy and looking pleased with herself. Then Mary went into the sitting room and switched on the answerphone. There would be few calls. Most people knew they were away, and in any case Lennox preferred his weekends free of work, so he discouraged all but urgent business.

It was the tone taken by Lettice which shocked Mary. 'Answer the phone, damn you . . . Where are you? Call me back right away. I mean, right now . . . We're at the flat, here's the number. As if you didn't already know it, you bastard . . .'

Automatically Mary scribbled down the numbers, the high-pitched voice piercing her ears. Then the phone must have been put down. But the messages continued, some still from an obviously distraught and angry Lettice, others in Tod Aumary's more moderate tone, coldly venomous. 'Answer this call now, Kemp . . . At once or you'll be sorry. What you've done is disgraceful, and you know it . . .'

There had been one further call from Lettice, early on Monday morning: 'I'm going to call your office, Lennox Kemp, and I don't care who hears what I have to say. No matter what you thought of us, you had no right . . .' The harsh voice trailed off into incoherence.

Mary sat still for a moment, staring at the machine, then she reached for the phone. No, she thought, all these calls were made in a rush of anger, and the last one meant there would be a message for Lennox when he reached the office. She withdrew her hand from the phone, and went into the kitchen to prepare dinner. The peremptory tones of both Lettice Aumary and her husband had put her back up; she would not jump to their bidding. She would wait until she heard from Lennox.

He also had sat quietly listening to Perry Belchamber's account of the call from Mrs Aumary which had come in that morning at nine thirty.

'It was more than Audrey at the switchboard could cope with. The woman rampaged on about how you were avoiding answering her calls. She insisted that you were in the office and refusing to talk to her. Audrey did the right thing, she remained polite, and said she would hand over the call to the most senior partner in the office. That happened to be me. I've taken a note, both of what she said to Audrey and afterwards what was said to me by both Mrs Aumary and her husband. I'm not taking any chances, Lennox, this was a vicious attack on you made over the phone.'

Kemp nodded. 'Thanks, Perry. At least Dr Aumary talked sense, though why he should blame me for the death of his brother-in-law defeats me. I can understand Lettice Aumary's distress also but not this personal attack.'

'Both of them insisted that you go out to this flat in Crownberry Avenue as soon as possible. Will you go? Might well be the best way to clear up what is obviously a misunderstanding.'

'Yes, I'll go immediately. Thanks, Perry, for diffusing the situation as far as the office is concerned, and for taking a note. Old habits die hard, eh?'

Perry Belchamber had practised at the Bar for years before opting for the less stressful life of a suburban solicitor. The note, in his quick, clear script, was an exact rendering of every word spoken on the telephone that morning.

'Watch your back, Lennox,' he warned as he got up to go. 'They sound as if they're out to make trouble for you.'

Kemp put the page torn from the notepad squarely on the desk in front of him, and tried to make some sense out of it.

What was clear, and naturally distressful, was that Roger Warrender had taken an overdose sometime on Saturday, and although he'd been rushed to the emergency unit at the local hospital immediately, efforts to revive him had been in vain, and he had died there later that night. These facts had been tersely related by Dr Tod Aumary to Perry Belchamber, who merely replied that he would inform Lennox Kemp of them as soon as he came into the office. They had at least made more sense than the rest of the words spoken.

Kemp found he had still retained the scrap of paper with the late Roger Warrender's telephone number, but he decided against phoning; he would simply do as he was asked, meet the Aumarys at the flat.

But first, to reassure Mary, for she must have already been a target for those previous messages from Lettice. He found her in the kitchen but knew as soon as she turned her face to him that she was already anxious.

'She never said he was dead, her brother I mean. She was just raging at you for some reason or another. What's it all about, Lennox?'

'Blessed if I know, and that's the truth. Let's listen to those calls.'

Even with the knowledge that Roger had died, and in dreadful circumstances, what Lettice was saying on the phone still made no sense to Kemp. 'She's blaming me for something, and so is Torvil – something I said, something I did . . .'

'Well, it couldn't have been on your first visit or she'd have told you in the car bringing you home,' said Mary, shrewdly. 'This temper of hers, it was more recent.'

'She must have been devastated by Roger's death – and the manner of it.'

'Did he seem suicidal to you?'

Kemp thought about it seriously for a moment, knowing the question was going to be vital. 'I would have said not,' he replied, finally. 'Of course Roger was unhappy. Who wouldn't be in his circumstances? But contemplating taking his own life? No.'

'And last Friday when you visited?'

'But I didn't see him. All Miss Maitland said was that he'd had a bad night, been given an injection, and was asleep. Certainly she did mention liver failure or something of the sort. I'm no expert, but it could have meant a grave worsening of his condition. If that was the case, why wasn't he in hospital?'

'We're just going round in circles. Although I don't want you to go and see them, it might be for the best.'

Kemp was already putting on his coat; it was much colder in London than it had been in Ireland. He suddenly felt a pang, sorrow for a lost time . . .

Mary went to the door with him, and seemed reluctant to let him go.

'This won't take long,' he assured her.

She gave him a quick kiss, and then stepped back, surprised at herself, but all she could say was: 'Be careful, darling. I don't like these people.'

Well, I don't much like them either, Kemp thought as he drove away. Instead of taking this ridiculous journey into Outer London he should be either putting in an hour or two at the office or sharing happy playtime, bathtime and bedtime with young Elspeth.

It was hard to prevent a build-up of resentment though he struggled against it by giving a thought to Roger, a man he had not liked but with whom he sympathized. A man he would never speak to again. What had made Roger take his own life at this particular juncture?

He thought back to meeting him at the flat with Lettice. He did not have total recall of what had been said – the occasion did not at the time seem to warrant it. How long had they been in Roger's company? At most, two hours. What had been said? Nothing of consequence. He remembered he'd thought the scene stagey. Was it before or after he'd mentioned the name of Perce Cavendish that Roger had scribbled 'Come alone'?

But it was Roger who had asked to see Kemp even before that. Could it have been, as Mary had joked, to apologize for that long-ago beating? Was that all there was to it, penitence and absolution? Somehow Roger Warrender didn't seem to be the type. But a dying man's need for confession . . . Kemp pulled himself up just as he braked hard as a rogue van changed lanes. Did Roger Warrender know he was dying? Did he take the quick way out on his own terms rather than hang on under onerous medical supervision?

The afternoon had been murky, and by the time he reached Crownberry Avenue the daylight had almost gone. This time he took the car right up to the door. The lamp had not yet been lit, and the place smelt of old, damp stone. One pull at the Gothic bell chain and the door was opened swiftly by Tod Aumary, who said nothing, but stepped aside to allow Kemp to enter.

Two can play at that game, Kemp thought as he divested himself of his coat and threw it over the back of a chair. So, he too remained silent and it was Lettice, thrusting herself forward from the sitting room, who had the first word.

'At least you've come,' she said, curtly, 'but you've avoided it for long enough.' She turned on her heel and went into the room ahead of the two men. There was a tea trolley with half-empty cups, and an uncut sponge cake. Kemp didn't think he was going to be offered anything. In fact Torvil pushed the trolley to one side with his foot as he made his way to the big chair in which Roger had sat on Kemp's last visit. Lettice sat herself carefully on the edge of the sofa, looking more like an irate headmistress than ever. Nobody asked Kemp to sit down.

Nevertheless, he took the remaining chair, and decided not to waste any more time.

'I'm really very sorry to hear about Roger. You must both

be very distressed by the manner of his death, but I do not see why you have involved me.'

Lettice made a sound of contempt, something between a hiss and a snarl, but it was her husband who spoke, cold and incisive.

'You involved yourself, Kemp, when you brought him that bottle of whisky.'

Kemp looked, and felt, utter bewilderment. 'What bottle of whisky?'

Lettice swivelled round, nodding her head at Torvil. 'I told you he'd deny it . . . And he was always a good liar.'

Torvil got up as if he was more at ease talking on his feet. He took a turn about the room before coming to a halt in front of Kemp. 'You came here last Friday afternoon, completely unannounced. You pushed your way in, despite Miss Maitland telling you that Roger was asleep, and then, because you couldn't get to see him you deliberately left him that bottle of Scotch in the loo, where you knew he'd find it. By so doing, you delivered the means whereby Roger could take his own life.' There was a catch in his throat when he got to the end. He turned abruptly away from Kemp and walked across to the window, staring out at the grey dying of the light. Lettice was sobbing, and making no attempt to hide it.

Kemp was thinking rapidly. It was like being on his feet in court when a witness throws a spanner in the works by changing his story mid-trial.

'This is a lot of nonsense,' he said, because that was the first thought in his mind.

Dr Aumary came back from his contemplation of the damp shrubbery, and again stood over Kemp. 'You can't deny you came here?'

'Of course I came here on Friday afternoon. As Lettice knows, her brother had asked to see me, he'd given me his telephone number. I happened to leave London early, which was totally unexpected, and I phoned to see if it was all right to come. Miss Maitland did appear somewhat flustered on the phone, but she didn't tell me not to come. It was only when I got here she explained. Of course I quite understood that Roger couldn't possibly have visitors, and I left. That's all there was to my visit.'

'That's just not true.' Lettice was glaring at him with her red-rimmed eyes. 'You'd even been drinking before you came . . . You made an excuse to Miss Maitland that you wanted to use the toilet, and she – the poor woman was already distressed enough by your appearance, your rudeness – she showed you in there.'

Lettice pointed in the direction of the door at the end of the sitting room.

'I bet you knew just where exactly to hide the bottle you were smuggling in for poor Roger,' said her husband. 'That's where he used to stash his supplies until Miss Maitland found out and I gave her permission to keep searching the flat, if necessary every day.' He paused for a moment. 'Did Roger ask you to bring it in? It doesn't really matter if he did. You're a professional man, you must have some knowledge of alcoholics, you would know how desperate they can get . . .'

'It was the cruellest, most despicable act I've ever known!' Lettice burst out. 'It was like handing him poison. Oh, I know now how you must have hated him for what happened all that time ago. Yes, Torvil has told me. In the light of what you did to Roger he thought it best I should know that they'd both assaulted you once. But to take your revenge like this – it's monstrous.' Lettice lay back in her chair, exhausted by her words, and the strength of feeling behind them.

Kemp addressed her husband. 'Dr Aumary,' he said, keeping his voice level, 'I don't know how you've come up with this story that I deliberately brought a bottle of whisky into this flat for Roger. Only a complete idiot would do thing like that, and idiot I am not. Yes, I did use the loo in the very short time I was here. Miss Maitland kindly showed me where it was. I was cold and wet . . .'

'And you'd been drinking,' said Torvil, flatly. 'Miss Maitland knew that. The smell was on your breath.'

Kemp did some more quick thinking. He had in fact forgotten because it hadn't seemed important at the time, but while in Counsel's Chambers once they knew the trial would not go on that day, yes, he'd had a small whisky with Jeremy Young while they discussed another appointment.

It had only been a quick swallow from a tiny glass; surely that could never have been detected an hour or so later by Miss Maitland? Or had he, so horrified by his dishevelled appearance in the hall mirror, muttered something to her about having had a drink to keep out the cold? He could not honestly remember much of their conversation apart from the fact that there had been a lot of apologizing for no apparent reason other than he had caught it from her.

Unfortunately his present momentary hesitation was pounced on by both his listeners anxious, it seemed, to wrong-foot him at every turn.

'You were drunk,' said Lettice, disgust driving her voice, 'and you decided to get your own back on Roger by getting him drunk, too.'

'Of course I didn't.' Kemp was beginning to get angry. 'I was only in this flat five minutes last Friday. I neither saw Roger nor did I bring anything in for him. Surely Miss Maitland can confirm that.'

'You did a lot of damage in five minutes,' said Tod Aumary, coldly, 'and I don't know how you have the nerve to impugn Miss Maitland.'

'Is she here in the flat? I would like to see her if she is.' Although it would be normal practice for a housekeeper to move on when there was no longer anyone to housekeep for presumably Miss Maitland would still be around – if only to clear up this nonsense about his visit last Friday.

'Poor, poor Millie,' Lettice murmured. 'What a terrible time she has had. And now this . . .' She turned fiercely on Kemp. 'Why can't you be man enough to admit it? Just a stupid prank. You were a bit tipsy, you didn't think it through . . . But at least spare us – and Millie – your lies.'

Her brother laid a restraining hand on her arm. 'Calm down, Lettice,' he said. 'When Kemp hears what Miss Maitland has to say he'll change his tune, you mark my words. I'll have her in and he can listen.'

Aumary got up and crossed to the door, and opened it. The housekeeper couldn't have been far away since she was quickly over the threshold. She walked stiffly to the centre of the room and acknowledged Kemp's presence by a nod in his direction, but without meeting his eyes.

Eleven

When Kemp revisited the scene in his mind – which he was to do many times in the coming days – the dominant figure was Millicent Maitland centre stage in the plush green-and-gold drawing room, an avenging angel in blue serge skirt and flat-heeled Hush Puppies, not a wisp of hair astray round her little beak of a face. Indeed it may well have been as that figure she saw herself, secure in the path of righteousness.

She refused the offer of a chair brought forward by Lettice, whose attitude to the housekeeper was of one guarding some precious object. 'I prefer to stand,' said Millicent, briskly. 'I'll be taking the trolley out in a minute anyway. But you wanted to see me, Doctor?' She turned her slightly protuberant eyes on the person in the room whom she would necessarily assume to be in charge.

'I'm afraid I have to trouble you once again to go over that visit of Mr Kemp's last Friday, Miss Maitland. Unfortunately he doesn't seem to realize . . . Well, the point is that he's not being completely frank with us . . .'

There was a short, uncomfortable silence as Miss Maitland turned a bland and mildly astonished gaze on Kemp.

When she did speak her voice was soft, as gentle as a cooing dove.

'But surely you remember, Mr Kemp, how you came here completely out of the blue? I was so startled at first that I nearly didn't let you in, but it was raining so hard and you were soaking wet. You didn't seem to understand what I was telling you – that you couldn't see Mr Roger because he was asleep. I tried to tell you that the doctor had been to give him an injection and that he wasn't to be disturbed, but you pushed past me . . .'

'I did not push past you, Miss Maitland. I understood exactly what you were telling me, that Mr Warrender had had a bad night, that there had been a downturn in his condition and that, naturally, he could not be visited that afternoon. Had you told me all this on the phone I would not have called at the flat.'

A tiny frown appeared on the bland forehead. 'I don't know what you mean about the phone, Mr Kemp.'

'I telephoned a short while before I came. I did not arrive "out of the blue" as you put it. I telephoned to explain that I had found myself in the vicinity due to unexpected circumstances and that I would come and see Mr Warrender as he had asked me to. You told me nothing on the phone to prevent my calling.'

Miss Maitland shook her head slowly from side to side in disbelief, and appealed to the other listeners. 'Why is he talking about a phone call? There was no call to this flat that afternoon. Of course he may have rung while I was busy in the washroom – there were sheets, there was soiled linen to be taken care of – and I may not have heard. If I had taken such a call, of course I would have told him that a visit that day would have been untimely. After the doctor left and we had got Mr Roger asleep, there was a lot to do and I was upset by the change in my patient's condition . . .'

She broke off and looked to Lettice, who bounded forward with a protective arm. The reference to the sordid details of the work she did as nurse rather than as housekeeper brought murmurs of sympathy from both the Aumarys.

Kemp, who was beginning to get angry at what he felt was a charade, recognized it as a neat move on Miss Maitland's part in the game.

She put Lettice's arm gently from her shoulder. 'It's all right. I can go on. As I was saying, had he telephoned of course I would have told him not to come. When the doorbell went it would have been about four in the afternoon and I was just crossing the hall from the kitchen. I was startled because no one was expected, and then his appearance, well, I very nearly didn't let him over the door.' She turned and looked fully at him. 'You must admit you did look rather odd. Like a dying duck in a thunderstorm. I was so sorry for you and let you in, and you were dripping water all over the hall.'

The old-maidish expression so neatly fitted exactly what Kemp had felt himself to be that Friday afternoon, a dying duck in a thunderstorm, that for the moment he could almost believe Miss Maitland's version of his visit.

'And then you asked if you could use the toilet,' she went on, implacably. She gave a small laugh, as she turned to the others. 'I wasn't surprised. It was very cold out, and he said he'd had a drink before leaving London, to "keep out the cold" he said. Of course I couldn't do other than offer him the facilities, and I showed him the downstairs toilet. It must have been then, Dr Aumary, that he left that bottle. I never looked, but of course I never dreamed . . .' For the first time, Millicent was flustered. 'All those times I used to search it in case Mr Roger – Oh, I shouldn't say it now . . .'

'That's OK, Miss Maitland. You did a wonderful job with him, and we've a lot to be thankful for what you did. There was no way you would know of the trick someone else was going to play on poor old Roger.'

It was the false commiseration in the words 'poor old Roger' that grated on Kemp rather than the more sinister aspects of what was becoming a horror story with himself at the centre. Well, he had politely listened. Now, with a rougher edge to his tongue, he rounded on Tod Aumary.

'Suppose you tell me what brand of whisky was it that I left, according to Miss Maitland?'

The Doctor's response came rapidly. 'A large Teacher's, as you well know. It was found by Roger's bedside table. He'd used it to help him to swallow all the paracetamol tablets he'd managed to accumulate. God knows how long he'd been thinking of suicide but that damned bottle of Teacher's took him over the edge. He simply couldn't resist his favourite tipple – and you left it where he'd be sure to find it . . .'

'Oh, don't, Torvil, please . . .' Lettice was openly sobbing, and her husband paused.

Miss Maitland, on the other hand, found strength to take up the tale.

'Dr Aumary and I found the label from the bottle on the floor of the downstairs toilet on Saturday evening after Mr Roger had been taken into Emergency. He had got up that morning saying he felt better after a good sleep, and he sat in the drawing room for a while reading his paper . . . He must have gone to the toilet and found the bottle . . . Oh, if only I'd known he had it! But I hadn't the least suspicion. Dr Aumary knows how careful I have been to see that there is never any liquor in the house!' She was looking directly at Kemp now, her hands clasped in front of her at rest, one upon the other; he could see no sign of nerves nor agitation.

'I'll just take the trolley out,' she said, turning to Lettice. 'I thought maybe a cup of tea . . . But, I understand now. This man is saying he never brought in that bottle when we all know he did. Perhaps he only meant it as a joke . . .' By this time she was at the door and her voice almost unheard under the clatter of the trolley wheels on the bare parquet where the carpet ended. She closed the door softly behind her.

'I don't know what's going on here,' said Kemp, 'but what she says is nonsense. I telephoned and spoke to her on the phone last Friday. I came to the flat, she told me then that I could not see Roger, and I left.'

'You went in there.' Lettice gave an angry nod in the direction of the further door. 'And you left a bottle of whisky.'

'I went to the loo, yes, but I didn't leave anything in there.'

'You had it in the pocket of your overcoat. Millie said there was something bulky in your pocket when you bumped into her at the drawing-room door. Why are you denying everything? Is it just because you know you were drunk at the time?' Lettice by now was fierce. Dr Aumary was cold, implacable and distant.

'I think we've heard enough from you, Kemp, and I would be glad if you would leave us. You will be told the date of the inquest. Naturally, questions will be asked.'

Twelve

Mary Kemp had listened in silence to her husband's rather sketchy account of this third visit to the flat in Wanstead, or, as she put it herself, the domain of the Warrender–Aumary faction. Being scrupulous, however, she admitted to prejudice.

Though not by birth an American – it had happened in Ireland for which she remained unreasonably grateful – Mary Blane Kemp was so by upbringing and allegiance. Domiciled now in England, a country which she was studying and starting to like, there were still many aspects of the English that rankled. Their sense of property, for instance, as acres of rolling countryside rather than hard-won homesteads, and their hierarchy of social status seemed to her somehow stuck in an older world, based on the same principles as had governed them in the eighteenth century. There was still that deference to those above, and an only-just veiled contempt for those below . . . Of course she knew many English people who had none of these attitudes, and she had made many friends who would have been appalled had she voiced such views. It was the Warrender and Aumary families that got up her nose, even though she'd only met two of them.

It was somehow the whole 'idea' of them: what she'd heard about them and their lost lands, the fact that feeling let down by their own country they'd opted for America, where, in certain sections of society, their ancestry would pay dividends if not in power or profit but in status . . .

Thinking it over, she decided she was getting in too deep. She simply didn't like them. Dr Tod had been so gracious to her at that dinner party even when she'd told him her knowledge of the wealthy families on Long Island or New Hampshire was only through her nursing – only by a flicker of the eyes had she realized that in the latter part of their conversation he was making an effort to be nice. A lifetime of quiet observance of other people's foibles had made Mary a person of perception despite her rather frumpish looks and small stature.

As to Lettice, well, her feelings were mixed. Despite Lennox's slavish adherence to the uncle–niece relationship he believed they'd had in the past, Mary thought there was more of the snobby mother about the grown woman. That she had turned so vindictively upon Lennox now was no great surprise to Mary; Lettice Warrender as a girl may have had a deeper attachment to him than he'd realized then, and now.

With a woman's clearer perception Mary recognized that the young Lettice Warrender might have harboured romantic yearnings; finding them misplaced might well have soured the milk in later years.

The Kemps had finished dinner. When Mary brought coffee to the sitting room, her husband was prowling around, restlessly. 'Have you got total recall of either of these two visits to Roger's flat?' she said, pouring out their cups. 'Could you make what you used to call verbatim reports on them, what was said, by whom, and in what manner? And for heaven's sake, come and sit down.'

Kemp complied, ran his fingers through his hair, and thought about it.

'About what happened this afternoon, yes, because I knew it was important, and I did note every word spoken. But, last Friday – well, that's quite different. It wasn't a planned call, and I really wasn't concentrating on Roger at all. Let me put the thing in perspective: I was annoyed at not getting the full hearing that Jeremy Young and I had expected in the Chancery Court. It had been young Franklyn's case and I was only there to tidy up loose ends because he'd gone off to Ireland to prepare for the wedding. Yes, I suppose I was mildly irritated not to finish the business that day. I went back to Chambers with Jeremy, and, yes, we had a quick dram. Only because I wanted to ask him where I could buy that special single malt that we wanted to take as a gift to Dinah's Dad. Jeremy told me of a nearby wine shop and before I went to get my car I bought that bottle of Lagavulin which we took to Ireland.'

'And you put it in your overcoat pocket?'

'Yes, I slipped it in my pocket, still in its wrapping, and only took it out on Friday evening when I gave it to you to put with the presents we were taking for Dinah.'

'So it was in your pocket when you went to visit the late Roger?'

'It must have been, though I don't remember. And then according to Lettice, Miss Maitland caught sight of it when she was showing me into the sitting room on the way to the loo.'

'You didn't explain this to Dr and Mrs Aumary?'

'I had quite forgotten I had that bottle of single malt – and now it's become the deadly Teacher's . . .'

'Anything else about that Friday visit that you might have forgotten at the time but now recall?'

'You sound just like two detectives of the NYPD questioning a suspect, and not believing a word he says.'

'Well, that's just how I want to handle this investigation,' said Mary, airily. 'I've been on the wrong end of many of them and I know how it's done. How long were you in this downstairs toilet – as they call it?'

Kemp thought back, and tried to describe the place to her as he recollected it in his mind. There was a short, dark corridor and then the door into the loo. Clean but not particularly cheerful, there had been an ancient washstand with a mirror, and set out on the marble top a soap dish, tooth mug and shaving kit. On the open shelves below were toilet rolls, and towels behind which it would have been easy to stash a bottle or two.

'Which was what I was thinking at the time,' he explained to Mary, 'because on my first visit I was sure that Roger had taken a quick pick-me-up while going to the loo. It was a natural thought on my part when I was actually in the place. But I was hardly there three minutes, I was only too anxious by then to be out of the place and on the way to a dry home. I was conscious of dripping all over the linoleum in that loo so I certainly wasn't going to linger.'

'Funny that the tidy Miss Maitland didn't rush into that toilet to clean the floor after you'd gone,' said Mary, thoughtfully.

'That hadn't occurred to me before, but I see your point. From today's conversation I couldn't get a clear picture of the exact sequence of events on the Saturday morning. Apparently Roger was well enough to get up and go into the sitting room, and they presumed he went to the loo, where he found he'd been visited by the Easter Bunny, who'd left him an egg . . .'

'Don't joke, Lennox, I'm trying to get some kind of sequence in my mind, too. Where were his loving kin at this time?'

'Of that I can't be sure. All Miss Maitland had said to me was that she had informed them that Mr Roger had taken a turn for the worse, and they would get there as soon as they could. I think – but of course I can't be certain – that Tod Aumary was in Edinburgh. Lettice could have been with him or simply at their hotel in London.'

'So you don't know?'

Kemp sighed. 'There are many things I don't know, the

whereabouts of Roger's kin is merely one of them. As to
that Friday afternoon, it's still vague in my mind because
I never thought I'd have to remember it in such detail, and
also because the weekend in Ireland intervened, as it were.
A whole different place, new people to meet, a happy, incon-
sequential time, it's had the effect of rubbing out the Friday
afternoon's visit – well, it never really went into my memory
in the first place.'

'It's certainly different from Miss Maitland's account.'

'Except in the essentials; I did go there at the time she
says but only after a phone call she says never took place,
I was rather wet when I appeared at her door, I was rather
apologetic because I hadn't taken in what she'd said on
the phone . . . When I understood that Roger was sleeping,
I left. Oh, you see, I've already forgotten, I did go to the
loo . . .'

'Can you remember exactly what you said to her about
that?'

'I think I said, "Would you mind if I used your loo . . ."
And something about having left London in a hurry.'

'And what did Miss Maitland say today?'

'Oh, that's clear enough: "Then you asked if you could
use the toilet." And those were her exact words.'

'Well, she certainly got that wrong,' said Mary, with some
satisfaction.

'How can you be so sure?'

'In all the years I've known you, Lennox, you've never
used the word "toilet" – even when we're talking about
Elspeth, it's always the bathroom, or the loo, never the
toilet.'

Kemp laughed, for the first time that day. 'You'd make
a great detective, Mary, because you actually do listen to
what people say . . . You're quite right. In our house the
word was never used. My mother, who aspired to gentility,
thought it common, and of course the minor public school

I was sent to aspired to be Winchester, so there the word was absolutely forbidden. How very smart of you to notice.'

'I'm studying the English and their manner of speaking,' said Mary. 'It's all part of my late education. I can see that "toilet" would be a word used by the likes of Miss Maitland herself but not by you. I know it doesn't prove anything, but it should be noted. Now I would like to know about the time between the phone call you made and you landing on the doorstep.'

'I sat back in the car, and waited for her to call back. Five minutes, nearly ten . . . I thought she wasn't going to call, I nearly just drove off.'

'Pity you didn't . . . When you were at the flat could there have been anyone else there?'

'Well, I was only in the hall, that downstairs loo, and crossing the sitting room. To tell you the truth, I did wonder when she left the phone whether she had gone to speak to someone . . . I don't know why I had the thought. Certainly she was not altogether with it, if you know what I mean. She had been flustered on the phone, and not very coherent, and when I arrived she still seemed a bit distrait. I put it down to my appearance, all wet and looking like a tramp. And that damn bottle in my coat pocket, it must have weighed it down . . . She seems to have told Lettice that I bumped into her by the drawing-room door. If you ever meet our Millicent Maitland you'll see she's not the kind of person you bump into. She certainly opened the door for me, and then stood aside, all starchy and stiff. I swear I never touched either her or her very respectable clothing.'

'What was she wearing?'

'Something old-maidish and with sensible shoes, flat-heeled. Much the same as today, which was crisp white blouse, blue serge skirt and Hush Puppies.'

'Well observed, but then you had more reason today to note everything about her appearance.'

'Too right I had. I was watching for just the least flicker of unease, the smallest bit of shiftiness, the nervous hand to the mouth, all the usual signs when someone is lying through their teeth – as she was. Can we close this interview now, please? I'd like a large brandy.'

Thirteen

Worried though he was by what he hoped could only be a wrong interpretation of his involvement with the late Roger Warrender, Kemp got on with next day's work, settling client matters and keeping the firm of Gillorns firmly on an even keel.

Joan Wheatcroft came into his room as he was signing the mail.

'You remember you said you'd like to meet my gran, Mr Kemp? Well, I'm going out there on Saturday.' She paused. 'Feel a bit guilty, really – haven't been to see her for weeks, what with the wedding and getting myself an outfit for it . . .'

'And very nice you looked, Joan. Some of those Irish lads were quite impressed.'

'They're a lot smarter than they look,' she said seriously, 'and I've already had one telephone call . . . Sorry, didn't mean to go on so. It was just to ask if you really meant . . .'

'Of course I did. If this good weather holds, we'll make it a family outing. Mary and I will pick you up – about two?'

'That'll be great, Mr Kemp. I'll give Gran a ring. She likes having someone to talk to about the past, and for an old person she can be real fun.'

'That's a date, then, Joan. Here, take this lot out to the post table.'

After the office closed Kemp made several attempts to phone Dr Sutherland, without success.

'I was sure I had him on the line at least once,' he told Mary over dinner, 'but there seemed to be a glitch in the connection . . . What's up?' he asked her when he noticed she was looking uncomfortable.

'I wasn't going to tell you,' she replied, hesitantly, 'but I had a bad experience in the supermarket this morning. I saw Marion across the aisle – we generally shop about the same time – and gave her a wave, but got no response. I was close to her again at the checkout, and said hello . . . She turned her head away, pretended to be looking in her handbag . . . But it was obvious that she simply wanted to ignore me . . .'

Kemp felt a rising anger. He knew that Mary valued the friends she had made in the district, and this encounter had clearly disturbed her. He decided that some action on his part was necessary . . .

'This nonsense must be stopped before it gets too serious and I start losing clients. I'll go round tonight and see Jim Sutherland.'

'Perhaps he won't see you, Lennox. Tod and Lettice Aumary are old friends of the Sutherlands, aren't they?'

'Not exactly. Dr Sutherland had his surgery here when I arrived over twenty years ago but his relationship with the Warrender family at that time was only professional. Paula didn't mix with local doctors – not quite their sort, she would say – no more than she mixed with local lawyers like me. They used us when we were needed, like they used their land agents to collect rents from the tenantry or the local vicar to baptize the servants' infants. But they went to Harley Street consultants, and City law firms when their own personal concerns were involved. But I've known and liked Jim for twenty years and he's not going to get away with listening to only one side of the story. Besides,' Kemp added, with a grin, 'he owes me . . .'

'Of course. You and Franklyn Davy solved that case where his young partner almost got away with murder.'

'That's what I mean, he owes me. No, keep the coffee till I get back. I shan't be long, but what I do want from Jim is some idea of exactly how Roger Warrender came to die. I simply can't get a grip on this thing till I get hold of facts, timetables, the whereabouts of certain folk, when he was taken to hospital, how long before he died . . . It's going to be worth any risk of being snubbed on the Sutherlands' doorstep if I can find out the things I want to know.'

'I suppose they will all come out at the inquest. Does there have to be one? After all, Roger was under close medical supervision, from what I've heard, and he did die in a hospital.'

'I rather think both Tod and Lettice would prefer any inquest to be as quick and inconspicuous as possible, he for the sake of his professional reputation – he made out that he was in charge of Roger's treatment – and she because you don't go around shouting about a brother who was an alcoholic, and possibly a drug addict. The fact that he was also gay was something the Warrender family managed to skate over pretty smartly twenty years ago. Nowadays, it doesn't matter the same, but I'm sure neither Lettice nor her husband would want to know who Roger's present friends might be, what grubs might crawl out of the woodwork if there was too much publicity over the death.'

'I didn't know Roger was gay. Nobody mentioned it.'

'You wouldn't expect it to be a conversational gambit at the Sutherland–Aumary dinner table. To me it never seemed relevant, but now I'm not so sure.'

He struggled into his overcoat, and tried to keep his temper from rising any further on the ten-minute drive to the Sutherlands' house. It was the retired doctor himself who came to the door and, as Mary had predicted, tried to shut it when he saw who was standing outside. Kemp went forward and put his foot into the aperture.

'I hate to do this, Jim, but, as they say in the sitcoms, you and I have to talk.'

Dr Sutherland didn't smile, but he did stand back and opened the door wider. 'Oh, you'd better come in. Marion's gone to her yoga class, otherwise I couldn't let you over the threshold. She's taken what Lettice said pretty seriously. Put your coat down. I'm not going to offer you a drink, but there's coffee.'

'Coffee's fine, though the other might be appropriate.' Kemp followed his host into the sitting room, where the sofa reminded him that not so very long ago he'd sat there with Lettice. This time he chose a straight-backed chair. Jim Sutherland busied himself with the percolator and cups, and didn't speak as if expecting the other man to make the first move.

'I've had a kind of interview with Tod and Lettice Aumary, and heard directly from their Miss Maitland what I'm accused of – namely, introducing into the house of an alcoholic a bottle of whisky, as a result of which, they say, Roger Warrender was enabled to commit suicide. The accusation is not true, though some of the facts are.'

Sutherland pulled out a small table and put down Kemp's cup on it. 'Sugar?'

'No, thanks. I want you to know those facts. I did go to see Roger Warrender last Friday, but I telephoned first. This is denied by Miss Maitland. I was in the flat for about ten minutes in all, during which she explained just why I couldn't see Roger. Before I left, I visited their downstairs loo. I left no bottle of whisky anywhere in the flat, though I did have a bottle of Lagavulin in my pocket – a present to my young partner's new father-in-law, and which was duly delivered to him in Ireland on Saturday, where Mary and I attended the wedding. When we returned on Monday morning we found ourselves under attack from both Lettice and Tod, and eventually were given the news that Roger had died on Saturday night in hospital.' Kemp sat back and took up his coffee. He knew Jim Sutherland was not a man given to interrupting – he had carefully listened to too many case histories for that.

Instead he looked long and hard at his visitor without speaking. Then he said: 'I'd like to believe you, Lennox, because this act they say you did is both ludicrous and totally alien to the kind of person you are. Now, as to what I know. We were telephoned early on Sunday morning by Lettice to say that Roger had died in hospital the night before. I was out for my morning walk at the time, so it was Marion who got the full force of the anger and resentment felt by both the Aumarys – Tod came on the line as well. What was said, a bit garbled by Lettice but very clear by her husband, is that they were both in Edinburgh last week but due back in London on Saturday. Miss Maitland had told them Roger had a bad turn on the Thursday night but as the local doctor – I think his name is Samson – had given him sedation there was no need for them to return sooner. Nor, it seems, did they rush round there when they got back to London but left it till about eight o'clock on Saturday evening. Apparently he had been all right during the day, got up for lunch and told Miss Maitland that he'd have an early night and didn't want to be disturbed. That would be about six. Tod Aumary looked in on his patient when they arrived at the flat at eight, and found him on the floor unconscious. He was rushed into Wallcross Emergency, where they tried all the normal resuscitation procedures without success. He died there about nine o'clock. According to what Tod Aumary told me when I phoned him later on Sunday, Roger had somehow managed to stash away about fifty paracetamol tablets – he'd been prescribed them at some time because of muscle pains –

which he'd washed down with a whole bottle of Teacher's whisky brought into the flat by Lennox Kemp when he'd visited on the Friday afternoon. Naturally, both he and Lettice were distressed and angry at the sequence of events, and they're blaming you for what they see as a stupid and thoughtless impulse, or as much worse . . . A lot worse . . .'

'Well, it would be, if it were true,' said Kemp, 'and I can only repeat what I've already told you – I did not leave a bottle of whisky at Roger's flat when I called last Friday. Tod Aumary mentioned an inquest. Will there be one?'

Jim Sutherland shook his head. 'I shouldn't think so. The hospital will have done the post-mortem by now, but there's little doubt as to what Warrender died of. As a matter of fact I know the pathologist at Wallcross who would have done the PM. I was going to phone her later tonight when she was home. Stay there, Lennox, and I'll make the call from the study.'

For some time Kemp sat in an uneasy silence, save for the slightly off-beat ticking from an ancient grandfather clock which sounded as if it were out of step with time. The artificial logs piled up in the hearth glowed softly and purred like a contented cat. The red eye of the television stared back at Kemp, unconcerned whether he lived or died.

He stirred restlessly in his hard chair, wishing he'd chosen one more amenable to his contours. He fervently hoped that Jim would return to the room before Marion got in from her class; it had been a long and tiring day and he was in no state to be confronted by a woman fresh from elevating exercise who believed him to be the type of person to hand out strong drink to a sick alcoholic.

It was because of such depressing thoughts that he sprang to his feet in relief when Jim Sutherland came back into the room.

'I spoke to my pathologist friend, Pamela Sturges. Yes,

the PM was done this morning, and yes, Roger Warrender died from liver failure as the result of the ingestion of paracetemol tablets and whisky, both in considerable quantities. I've put it in non-medical terms, Lennox, so you will understand. As he took them himself there's no doubt about it being suicide. One thing I will add, however, is that Roger did not have long to live anyway. He already had damaged kidneys, and a stomach so ill used that I doubt if he could have been saved, no matter what rehabilitation was forced on him.'

Kemp sat down again. 'I wouldn't mind another coffee, if you don't mind. I have to have a think in view of what you've told me.'

'Just between ourselves – ' Jim Sutherland turned away to the side table and poured coffee for two – 'Roger Warrender had attempted suicide before . . .'

'Recently?'

'A couple of months ago. Just before he went to that Priory place – in fact it was me who got him in there, once Torvil had appealed to me.'

'It wasn't only drink, was it?'

Sutherland sighed deeply. 'I'm afraid not. It doesn't matter saying it now, but Roger had been on cocaine for years. To put it bluntly, he was a drug addict, the alcoholism simply went along with it, as it often does. It was on one of Torvil's visits to this country that he discovered the state Roger was in, and came to me for help because I'd been on drug-addiction committees – all that sort of thing.'

'Did Lettice know – about the drugs, I mean?'

Dr Sutherland gave a short laugh. 'I'm afraid Lettice has become very much like her mother – she only believes what she wants to believe. In this case it was that Roger had a drink problem which, with the help of herself and her husband, would be curable. You must understand that, unlike Torvil, Lettice hasn't been in England since she went to live in America. It's Torvil who has been doing all the caring for her brother.'

'Of course, he and Roger were always close,' said Kemp, slowly, 'despite Roger's little foible.'

'If you mean his homosexuality, for heaven's sake say it, man,' Jim Sutherland upbraided him. 'Don't go all coy with the words like we all tended to do twenty years ago.'

'Sorry,' said Kemp, 'I wasn't sure just how open Roger himself was about such things. There was certainly no question of that when his mother was around. I notice you've reverted to calling Torvil by his original name, by the way. Has he been coming over fairly regularly lately?'

'I don't think the change to Tod suits him, there's always been too much of the aristocracy about Aumary. Yes, he's become quite a well-known figure – particularly in the world of diabetics. I've seen quite a lot of him in the last six months since he asked for my help with Roger.' Jim Sutherland glanced at his watch; he too seemed to think grandfather in the corner was past his prime. 'Marion will be home in about five minutes. Let me tell her your side of this business, Lennox.'

'Right,' said Kemp, getting to his feet. 'Thanks for believing me, Jim, I hope she'll do the same. That damned bottle of whisky!'

Jim handed him his coat. 'Well, it was in the flat by Saturday morning, and according to Miss Maitland only you had called – that's their story, but no, I think they're wrong.'

'According to Miss Maitland,' repeated Kemp, 'she's the book of the gospel. Well, even gospels are subject to interpretation. Just one more thing before I go, Jim. Was Roger Warrender's name ever linked with that of Perce Cavendish'?

'Good lord, Lennox, you still on about that man? What's got into you?' Sutherland had the outer door open by now and the face he turned to Kemp was one of utter astonishment. 'Yes, if you must know, there were rumours at the time but of course nobody said much – certainly not when Paula Warrender was about. That's Marion's car turning into our road,' he added, hurriedly. 'Good night, Lennox. Don't worry, we'll try and sort things out with the Aumarys. You can count on me.'

Kemp got into his car and drove off, flashing his headlights at Marion's car as he passed it at the gate. It seemed foolish to be running off rather than facing her but he'd had enough to think about for the moment; that hour spent with her husband had been an hour well spent.

Fourteen

Several days later Kemp remarked to his wife that he thought it was time they gave a dinner party.

She stared at him. 'But you don't like dinner parties! What you like is to have friends round for supper and a chat – which generally lasts till the early hours. I make the food, you help in the kitchen, choose the wines and the guests, and everybody seems to have a good time. Is that what you mean?'

'Whatever. Yes, that's roughly what I mean . . .'

'"Roughly", that's when you have a motive. You're intrigued by something that can't be dealt with at the office, so you want to try the social line. Now, isn't that more like it? Now who do you want this time?'

'Well, we haven't had John Upshire and Brenda for some months . . . Could you stand her for a few hours?'

'Of course I can. I'm not completely callous. And she can help me with a recipe I keep on getting wrong. She and I can retire to the kitchen and you and John can get on with whatever it is you're after. It's still the Fenwick murder, isn't it?'

'I've been looking at those diaries of Dr Ayre's again. There's been alterations on some of the pages for dates in August 1979 – around the time the little boy went missing, and then was found dead. Entries have been rubbed out, and then written over. They wouldn't signify if the rest of the diaries had similar, but they haven't. Dr Ayre was neat and meticulous in her diary records, except on this one occasion where there's evidence of what one might call fumbling, an attempt to alter an existing account with something else.'

'Want me to have a look?'

'You're probably more used to the way doctors record things than I am. Dr Ayre never mentions names, for instance, except for pharmaceuticals—'

'That's for the spelling. All doctors have the same problem when there's a new drug on the market. I wonder what the firms will do when they run out of names! Where have you kept all the stuff on Dr Ayre?'

'They're in the study. We'll have a look at them after dinner. Perhaps I'm making a mountain out of a molehill . . . It's just that Perce Cavendish was a patient of hers . . . He died of cancer in the prison hospital the month after he was arrested.'

Mary held the page up to the light, then took up the magnifying glass. 'I agree,' she said, 'there's been something written here, then rubbed out and another entry made on top of it. And the date is Monday, the 13th August 1979. The entry reads "80s". Now that's what Dr Enid wrote in for every Tuesday about once a month. I'd guess it meant that was the day she visited her over-eighties, so why in this particular month should she change it to the Monday?'

'You've had a look through the rest of that year?'

'Yes, and I can understand most of it though she uses abbreviations the way most doctors do, and wee hieroglyphics for dosages and what not, and just initials for people, and reminders of their addresses. But it's only on the one day there's been any rubbing out, and something over-written. It's not like her usual practice. Well, at least she got a well-earned rest that year.'

'What do you mean?'

Mary skimmed through the pages. 'See this entry for the following week? It says "South'ton, Cruise" and then the next three weeks are crossed out, with no entries. I bet she went off on holiday. Can I have a read of those newspapers again?'

'I got the back numbers of the *Gazette* from the local office. They give a fairly good account of the case for the whole of that August but stopped of course when the man, Perce Cavendish was charged. Then the matter would be submerged in sub judice while the police got on with building up their case. But they must have had enough evidence by the time he was arrested – what date was that?

Mary was busy reading. 'The issue for Thursday the 30th says that Perce Cunningham, a 47-year-old man of Threlfalls Cottage, Ember, had been charged with the murder. They didn't waste much time before they pounced, did they?

'John Upshire hinted that, although he'd no previous, there had been complaints of previous assaults on children, that would have been enough to alert them.' Kemp sighed. 'It could be one of those cases where they nabbed a suspect, and then began building a case.'

'But this suspect got away . . .'

'By God's grace – if you can call it that.' Kemp threw the newspapers and diaries back on to his desk top in irritation. 'I can't work this way, it's all bits and pieces. I haven't even got a decent sequence of the events in the case, never mind the statements made.'

'Which is why we're going to have the Upshires to supper some time next week so that you can scrounge an old police file out of John. Do you think it that easy?'

'No,' Kemp admitted. 'Not this file. I've already sensed John's reluctance about the case – possibly because it never came to trial, possibly because there was something personal to him about it . . . I don't know . . .'

'I'd like to forget the whole thing so that we can enjoy our family outing to Fernley Green Common tomorrow afternoon, but that, too, is connected. You're a bit obsessional, Lennox, on the subject of Perce Cavendish; I'm beginning to feel we've taken him in as a lodger . . .'

'I probably wouldn't have been so curious if it hadn't been for the name cropping up and people's odd reaction to it. Particularly from what you call the Warrender–Aumary faction.'

Mary considered for a moment. 'I can't get out of my head the venom in your little Lettuce Leaf's voice at that dinner-table when she said the words "perverts like Perce Cavendish". If there had been anything going on between that man and her brother she must have known about it. You keep talking about her as if she was some innocent girlie . . .'

Kemp demurred. 'Her feelings towards Cavendish were probably based on the inference that he might lead Roger astray – at least that would be the way she felt twenty years ago.'

'When she was in love with you?'

'Oh, come on, Mary, I've explained all that. It was a kind of hero-worship, or rather, anti-hero-worship, the kind of thing she'd met in books, the flawed man, the outcast or Philip Marlowe walking down his mean streets . . . It was all a romantic dream state, it had no basis in reality.'

'You've spent some time analysing it,' remarked his wife, drily, 'but I can see why she'd be ashamed of such memories and why she's turned bitter on you now. I bet she'll have some hard things to say at the inquest.'

Kemp shook his head. 'I don't think she'll get the chance. Any inquest is likely to be quietly conducted and folded away for the sake of Tod's reputation and Lettice's memory of her brother. The harm they can do me is to start up some kind of whispering campaign before they leave for the States. That's why I've got to nip it in the bud.'

When he thought about it as a lawyer should, it occurred to him that what the Aumarys were saying about him amounted to slander; he couldn't see himself going down that treacherous road though he might have to remind them of that view should they push him too far.

In the car next afternoon driving out to Fernley Green Common two of the occupants had Perce Cavendish in mind. Although neither of them had ever met him, the patch of meadowland on the edge of Ember Woods was where Rickie Fenwick had lived that hot summer twenty years ago. What the third occupant of the car was thinking as they went to pick up Joan Wheatcroft no one would ever know. Snugly packed into her car-seat Elspeth, one year and a bit old, gazed out with wide grey-blue eyes as the scenery raced towards her, spinning past, dissolving into light, shade, colour and form. Everything was new, and everything was being absorbed, gathered in and laid down in the tiny, expanding storehouse of her brain.

'Oh, what a poppet!' exclaimed Joan, climbing in beside her, 'I could eat you up . . . Can I take her for a walk on the Common when we get there?'

'You can come with me,' said Mary, 'that's why I've brought the pushchair. Then Mr Kemp can have a long talk with your gran – I think that's what he wants.'

'She'll love that. Mum says she talks too much, always did, but I could listen to her for hours – she's that funny . . . Puts folk in their place, Gran does. Mum used to tell her to button her lip, I suppose she was too sharp for some, but now she's old it doesn't matter any more – well, nobody has the time to listen.'

'How old is she, Joan, and what is her first name?' Mary felt it would not be right to address the old lady as Granny Wheatcroft, she believed in giving people their dignity.

'She's ninety-two, and she's called Alice . . . Funny,

that . . . I'd never thought of her as Alice. I wonder if it was from that book – *Alice in Wonderland*.'

'Or Alice Keppell, the mistress of King Edward the Seventh,' said Mary, with mischief in mind.

'Ooh, really? You mean like Prince Charles? I didn't know they had them in those days as well, Mrs Kemp. We never got that in our school history books.'

'Alice would be a common enough name about the time your granny was born,' Kemp said, quickly, stemming further revelations from Mary.

He knew she enjoyed the odd kick at the royal family; being Irish–American she liked to think she didn't have to follow the Brits in reverence to their monarchy. He felt she might have been reading the wrong history books and was rather out of date in modern attitudes, but he could see that Joan was impressed.

She giggled. 'That's the kind of thing Gran would say. She talks about the royals as if they were neighbours just down the road who'd gone to the bad . . . She was never the one to kow-tow to people, even them she worked for . . .'

'Would that have been the Courtenays at the Manor?' Kemp asked. Sycamore Cottage would have come under that demesne at one time.

'Not the Terrible Twins,' said Joan, referring to a local scandal which had rocked the countryside when she was growing up. 'Gran was at the Manor in Silas Courtenay's time – ages ago, and she left when she got married to the coachman – that would be my grandfather. I don't even know his name, she always calls him Wheatcroft. Isn't that strange?'

Kemp knew of other elderly women, mostly country folk, who did the same, and he'd often wondered if they even did it in bed.

It was a still, calm day of hesitant sunshine and Sycamore Cottage was looking very picture-book pretty in its garden of fading hollyhocks and autumn asters. Joan hurried in with her two great plastic bags. 'Gran's groceries from the supermarket,' she'd explained. 'Either Mum or I get them every couple of weeks. She don't eat much, though. A lot of it goes to the cat.'

Alice Wheatcroft came down the path to meet them when the pushchair had been disentangled, and Mary opened the gate for herself and Elspeth, who had decided to walk, a new activity which required much concentration for mother and child.

'Eh, but she's the bonny one! Come up, little sweetheart.' She had Elspeth scooped into her arms and into the house before, breathless, Mary could greet her. I wouldn't mind having that strength at ninety-two, she thought. Kemp followed her in. The small narrow passage was dark until they reached the large room at the back which was both kitchen and parlour and where a long window welcomed the sun.

There was half and hour or so of confused chatter while Joan made cups of tea and Elspeth showed off her new shoes. Staggering slowly across to the old lady, she reached the safety of the heavy skirt, and hung on, looking steadily up at the lined, brown face and the dark-blue eyes meeting her own.

There seemed to be an immediate affinity between them.

Alice Wheatcroft was small and bony, as if that was all that was left of a larger self. Kemp thought she was like a hazelnut – gypsy-brown and sharp-cornered. She looked as if she could live for ever. And there was no doubt, she could talk. Between she and her granddaughter, the room filled with their voices, rising and falling, with the occasional cackle of laughter from the old woman, and an answering giggle from Joan. In the course of it many of the inhabitants of Newtown, its council estates and its shopkeepers came in for a rare old going-over. Mary found herself almost helpless with laughter listening to the bits she understood; the rest came in accents too country Essex and too fast for her to understand.

Beyond the window sill, where geraniums bloomed scarlet and pink, the sunshine grew stronger, reminding her of the walk on the Common she had planned. The toddler was prised from her clutch on Granny Wheatcroft's white apron – worn in the old-fashioned style as part of dress rather than for work – and carried out happily by Joan, who, despite her continuous chatter, had washed up, put away the groceries and tidied the parlour. Mary could see that whatever secretarial skills the girl had, she would be an asset for simply keeping things in their right place.

Kemp was very comfortable in a cushioned wicker chair beside the window. Mrs Wheatcroft faced him in an old cane rocker which creaked when she moved.

'Joan tells me you're interested in the murder of yon wee boy all them years ago,' she said, without preamble when the others had gone. 'What a terrible thing that was, him so small . . . He was an angel, Mr Kemp, a right angel. Oh, he'd the looks, all them golden curls, and the sweetest face you'd ever see.'

'You remember exactly when it happened, Mrs Wheatcroft? Kemp asked, testing her.

'Near the end of that hot summer. We'd had nothing like it, all them days of sun, right into August. There was hay early, and the corn ripenin' fast. Wheatcroft had just got the boot – well, Mr Silas, he said he'd no need of a coachman any more, now he'd got a chaffoor – that's what he called the man he'd got to look after them cars. But I'll say this for the old man, he let us have this cottage, rent-free – ' she may have been grudging, but she gave people their due – 'while Wheatcroft was alive. When I lost him – be seventeen years now, though it don't seem a day – they let me stay on. But going back to that summer; we'd had that play

105

Perce Cavendish put on, out on the Common it was – in the last week of July . . .'

The way the old lady told it it was like flashbacks in a film, a re-run of time that brought images directly to the eye. Despite sometimes running down other byways in her mind, the narrative kept to a pretty straight line, even to the date.

'You asked the date, Mr Kemp, well it weren't them news-papers kept reminding me, for I allus knew well enough. Monday, it was, and the 13th August because it was my friend Marge's birthday. Marge Flitton, she lived over Ember and she'd be goin' on seventy that day, so I be taking her a cake I'd made and a few eggs – in them days I had hens out back, folks 'ud be right grateful for 'em during the war, I can tell you. I was for walking over that day even though it were hot, over the Common I'd be going, then the main road where there'd be a bus if I wanted . . .'

Kemp knew the way, both from personal experience in his car, but also because he'd studied the local Ordnance Survey map. A good half mile it would be across the Common, and half a mile up the road to Ember Village.

'Poor Marge, she be dead some years now, but that day she'd be lookin' out for me about four o'clock when she'd have the kettle on, so I left home around half two. As I come down the path I was in no hurry, pickin' dead heads off the roses and sortin' out a few weeds from the border, and when I come to the gate I looked over at Fernley Cottage like I allus used to do to see if Amy or the little boy's about . . . And I saw him there on their bit of lawn all dressed up in that cowboy outfit she'd bought him for Christmas. I waved to him, and the little darling, he swept off that furry cap he had and bowed . . . Allus at the play-acting, he was, our Rickie . . .'

She stopped, and wiped her eyes with a corner of her apron. Kemp felt his own eyes blur . . .

When she took up her story again her sprightly tone was gone as she relived that episode from her past.

'It were Marge's hubby ran me home,' she said, 'be around six o'clock, and there's a crowd of folk outside in the lane. When I got out the car Amy Fenwick herself comes runnin' over, and she's cryin' on my shoulder like her heart would break . . . Then someone tells me that Dominic's missing. But I saw him, I tells them, there in the garden, the sun on his hair . . . And later there's a policeman comes, Sergeant Cobbins – I'd known him since he were a lad – and I says the same. The many times I said it, Mr Kemp, it grew worse each time . . . They called it making a statement, to me it tore my heart for they were saying I was the last person to see him that day – or ever . . .'

What Kemp wanted was to take her back, step by step, every inch of the way despite the pain which was showing itself. He recognized that memory in re-enacting scenes can also bring feelings from hidden depth of consciousness which were present at the time but since submerged.

'When you were going up to the Common, Alice,' he said, gently, 'did you meet anyone?'

'Lawks no, man . . . Who'd there be? It's a quiet afternoon, too hot for any to be walkin' though I never minded it. I allus loved the summer days. As I used to say to Wheatcroft, I'd be right browned off in the winter.' Kemp was amused to hear the old wartime expression come so naturally. In her time she'd seen a lot of soldiers returned from the wars.

'Of course there were children at the bus stop on the main road, larkin' about as usual, but I didn't see no bus, so I walks on and I was in Marge's house before she's got the kettle on.'

Kemp edged her back to the Common. 'It's a bit of a climb between the hedges till you get up there from Sycamore Cottage on to the grassy stretch. Did you stop?'

'Oh, aye, I allus did . . . Path gets a bit rough, like, and dusty. I'd brush it off my shoes, and look back . . . Rest my legs, and look at the scenery.' She cackled, possibly at the idea of herself in other days, a sprightly woman but never too rushed to look around her.

'Do you remember what you were thinking?' That was something she had never been asked before but she considered it with proper gravity.

'I was hummin' a tune,' she said, slowly. 'It's a habit I have when I'm on my own and there's no one about to hear me. I know what it was that day . . .' She began to sing, softly as if only to herself:

> *'Summer suns are glowing,*
> *Over land and sea . . .'*

Her voice trailed off, and her eyes had their far-away look.

> *'Happy light is flowing,*
> *Bountiful and free . . .'*

Kemp astonished himself by finishing the verse. Where the words had come from and into his head he had no idea, but, searching in his memory in the same way as he had been doing with Alice, he saw a room of little chairs and a pile of dog-eared books. Sunday school. It couldn't have lasted long, that phase of his upbringing; his parents were not churchgoers, but the tune and the words had stuck.

He could see the old lady was pleased with him for she nodded approvingly.

'There's few know the words these days,' she said, 'but it's a lovely hymn and that's what was in my mind that day. Back down on the roofs of the cottages the sun it were so bright you could hardly see. And there's that flash of red between the hedges . . .'

'A flash of red? Where was that?'

'Why, along the lane between ours and Fernley . . .' She stopped, and for the first time was reluctant to go on. After a while she said: 'I told that Sergeant Cobbins, and the other big man who come later . . . They kept on about it . . .'

'It would be important to them,' said Kemp. 'Was it a car?'

Alice Wheatcroft shook her head. 'They kept sayin' it were "a vehicle" . . . And of course when Mr Cavendish got arrested they said it were his red van . . .'

It was strange to hear Perce Cavendish referred to in a proper style; no one else had done so. 'Did you know him, Mrs Wheatcroft?'

'Only to nod to, like. But he'd never pass without a word, allus the gentleman he was. There's some treat countryfolk as if we weren't there . . . But not Mr Cavendish, allus a bow and a Good Morning to you, Mrs Wheatcroft . . . I'll say that for him, no matter what others say . . .'

'You liked him?'

But Alice was not to be drawn on that one. 'I never knew the man, Mr Kemp, nor wanted to after they said what he'd done. That was a terrible thing he did. And he'd pretended to be so fond of Rickie, allus taking him to plays and such, and then putting on the Midsummer Dream thing on the Common with Rickie lookin' like the angel he was . . . And when he painted that muriel on the wall of the church hall, it's Rickie's face he puts on it . . .'

Kemp made no attempt to correct her, though the word amused him. He could see how it was with Granny Wheatcroft and the man Cavendish. She had liked him, thought well of him until 'they', the omnipotent police, magistrates and the whole judicial system had decided he was a murderer. She would not question it. For all her country smartness and quick brain she would never imagine that the fact she liked Cavendish as a person was important, and when everyone else had made up their minds as to his real nature she would accept their verdict . . .

He sensed that she was tiring, her shoulders slumped.

'The old church hall's gone now,' he said. 'I understand it was pulled down when the school went.'

She sighed. 'That development lot, they said there was no need for it. They built houses on the ground, they did. Now there's no place for folk to meet, save for that new community centre in Ember. Nasty piece of work, that is, nothin' like the old hall . . .'

'So Mr Cavendish's painting went too?'

'I used to go and look at it till my daughter stopped me. Where's the harm? I said. It's all that's left of the lad . . . But then they scrubbed it out.' She sat still for a moment in silence, staring out of the window at the fading light. 'The face of an angel, he had that day,' she muttered to herself, 'and the sun on his hair . . .'

A clattering in the hall signalled the return of the other visitors, and there was a bustle of activity while Joan got her grandmother supplied with supper 'when she'd be ready for it' – although she saw herself as a very modern girl, in this cottage Joan reverted to country phrasing.

Goodbyes were said, old Mrs Wheatcroft lingered over the child who clutched once more at her apron. Kemp disentangled the small fingers. 'Thank you,' he said, 'for all you've told me. I'm sorry to have awakened memories which are sad for you.'

But she was ready for him. 'Nay, Mr Kemp, these things are all in the past and nought can change them. When you're my age everything's in the past, good times and bad, they're all one . . .'

In the car he asked Joan about the painting that had been in the old church hall.

She laughed. 'And did she call it a "muriel"?' she asked. 'There's nobody in the family dared to tell her she'd got the word wrong – even my mother – so it's still the way she tells it. I can only just remember seeing it maybe the once. It was all along one wall behind the piano. I think it was done in crayons, pastels probably, and in lots of colours. I know now it was supposed to be the Forest of Arden, and there were fairies and elves, and right in front was a red-spotted toadstool where Rickie Fenwick was sitting as Puck . . . Now I'm not sure I appreciated it at the time, I might have been told about it later, but I do think I really remember his face, all bright and perky . . . But they soon had it scrubbed out when Perce Cavendish was arrested.'

'I think your grandmother liked him.'

'I'm told that a lot of people did before they knew what he'd done,' said Joan, wryly. 'But I'll say this for my gran, there weren't many folk she liked, she was choosy in her way. I think she's always been a good judge of character – but of course everyone can make a mistake.' she added, hurriedly, 'as she did over Cavendish.'

There was nothing Kemp could add. I'm working in the dark here, he thought, I have so little information to go on. If only I can persuade John Upshire to let me have a look at that old file, then I might get a better idea of what this character Perce Cavendish was really like. He was suddenly struck with the disturbing thought that if he himself died this very afternoon some people would remember him only as the blackguard who gave a bottle of whisky to a dying alcoholic . . .

111

Fifteen

Lennox Kemp heard nothing from the Warrender/Aumary faction – as Mary insisted on calling them – for some time, which should have brought him peace of mind. Instead, it irked him for he sensed things being said, or done, without his knowledge. He was further frustrated when Mary reported that the Upshires were away in the West Country.

'I'll have to get hold of that file by other means, then,' he said, impatiently.

'You've got bees buzzing in your head,' she said, 'and you're not going to be worth living with till you clear them out. What about some of your other contacts at Newtown police? Are you owed any favours there?'

He was, so he resolved to call in that evening and collect. In the meantime work was duly performed, and clients given his full attention as he pushed Perce Cavendish and Roger Warrender out of his head for the time being.

Eleven o'clock brought coffee and a rather flustered secretary. 'Sorry to bother you, but there's a man outside, been there for nearly an hour and won't take no for an answer when I tell him if he hasn't made an appointment, you can't see him this morning.'

'What's he like, Miriam? Has he been abusive?'

'Not yet, but I can see he's getting angry. He just says he'll sit there till you see him. The other clients keep looking at him but he takes no notice.'

'How many are there now?'

'There's only Mrs Edwards, she's come to sign her will – it's all ready for her.'

'I'll come out and get her – give me an opportunity to have a look at this chap. Did he give you a name?'

Miriam shook her head. 'He makes me nervous, just sitting there like a kettle about to boil.'

'Right, let's have a look at him.'

Kemp followed his secretary out to the waiting room, and greeted Mrs Edwards while his eyes took in the only other occupant, a large, thick-set man who glared at him from under bushy eyebrows, but said nothing. 'Do come in, Mrs Edwards,' said Kemp, stepping back. 'Miriam, will you bring someone with you to witness the signature – you know the routine.'

The procedure took no longer than fifteen minutes, and Kemp had just got back to his seat after escorting Mrs Edwards to the door when Miriam came in.

'I'm sorry,' she said, 'but he did give me a card. He wasn't on your appointments list. Here it is.'

A plain card, with only the name: Daniel Dempster. Kemp turned it over. There was a written message: 'Friend of Roger Warrender.'

'All right, Miriam. I've some telephone calls to make, and then I'll see him.'

The girl had only just left and closed the door behind her when it crashed open with the sound of splintered wood-work, and the burly man from the waiting room burst in. He strode across the room, swept aside the desk as if it were a cardboard box, and grabbed Kemp by the collar. He threw him to the floor, and poised above him with a raised fist.

'You bastard, I've a mind to kill you . . .'

'Stop right now . . .' Kemp had difficulty getting any words out. He tried to struggle but the man had him pinned to the floor with a hand the size of a leg of lamb while the huge thumb and fingers fastened on his throat.

'You'd choke, see? Just like that.' Kemp felt his windpipe being squeezed; he couldn't swallow. With a great effort he kicked out, and caught the man's leg, knocking him temporarily off balance. The pressure eased for just long enough for Kemp to wriggle to one side, and try to get up before he was attacked once more. This time Dempster got both hands on the lapels of Kemp's jacket, and hauled him to his feet, then threw him down on his chair. 'You and your stupid tricks,' he snarled, bringing his face within an inch of Kemp's own, 'you killed Roger . . .'

Fortunately, the office premises at Gillorns were modern with partition walls, and certainly not soundproof. With a squawk of its broken hinge the door was thrust open by Mike Cantley and Franklyn Davey, who had heard the noise, and wondered what dissatisfied client was trying to break up their building.

Being the younger and the more athletic, it was Davey who floored the man Dempster by a sort of rugby tackle, concentrating on the knees as being the weakest area of a very large man. Cantley came over and held him down, while he and Franklyn looked at Kemp. He'd had some rough customers in his office before, but this one had gone too far.

'Police?' Cantley queried, tersely. 'Not just yet,' said Kemp. 'Can you get him up and into the visitor's chair and we'll see what he has to say.'

Between them they hauled Daniel Dempster to his feet and pushed him into the armchair opposite Kemp. Then they both stood back,

Kemp nodded. 'In private,' he said.

'I'll be within call,' said Mike Cantley. He had been with Gillorns as conveyancing clerk and legal executive for as long as the firm had been in Newtown, and he had experienced many of Kemp's cases in the past which went beyond those of the usual suburban lawyer. He trusted his boss to handle this one on his own if that was what he wished. Franklyn Davey had not been with Kemp so long, but he valued him as a friend; he'd taken the measure of the big man and would like to have remained, but to this suggestion Kemp shook his head.

'A client deserves confidentiality,' he said, 'even if his manners are a little rough.'

When they were on their own, Kemp straightened his collar and tie, and addressed his visitor severely.

'First,' he said, 'I see you call yourself a friend of the late Roger Warrender . . .' As the man called Dempster began to speak, Kemp held up his hand. 'You'll get your turn. Just shut up and listen to me. Whatever you may have heard, I did not bring whisky into Roger's flat, I paid two visits there, one in the company of his sister Mrs Aumary, and one on my own when I did not see Roger. That is the full extent of my knowledge of the place. I knew Roger Warrender slightly when he was a young man twenty years ago, and I had never seen him since. I was told by Dr and Mrs Aumary that he had become an alcoholic, and when I did see him on that first visit I could well believe it. I understood he was very ill. I repeat once again, I did not take any drink into that flat.'

Mr Dempster may have been quick with the fisticuffs, but he appeared to be somewhat slower in his wits. He stared at Kemp with eyes of a dark-brown colour which showed no spark of light. He was a man of good complexion, even a reddish tan on his cheekbones as if he had spent some time in the open air. He seemed to be taking in very slowly what Kemp was saying, and then putting it under his own scrutiny, so that when Kemp had finished speaking there was a moment's silence.

Dempster said: 'I was told by all of them that you brought

115

Roger a bottle of Teacher's. Why would they say that if it wasn't true?'

'Good question, to which at the moment I haven't the answer.'

'Why should I believe you? You're not even a relative. They're family, and respectable people. Mrs Aumary said you did it in revenge. You wanted to pay off an old score. A stupid prank that went wrong. Why didn't you own up?'

Daniel Dempster spoke in short sentences that would have had Hemingway shooting his boots off in delight, but Kemp took back what he'd thought originally, that the man was slow-witted; he was in fact a slow thinker, one who took his time with ideas and putting them into words. He was certainly not an easy conversationalist, which made Kemp wonder about his occupation. He had a shrewd guess as to his relationship with the late Roger but it must have been deep and enduring enough to account for his initial outburst of temper.

'For the present, Mr Dempster, you will simply have to take my word for it that I did not do what the Aumarys say I did. Now that you have calmed down, I see no reason why we shouldn't discuss other matters sensibly.' Kemp glanced at his watch, and noticed that the other man did the same, exposing the tattoo of a ship on his hairy forearm. Merchant Navy, decided Kemp; that would account for the taciturnity – long days at sea – and the overall healthy look.

'About this time,' he said, 'I generally have a bite of lunch sent in or I visit the local pub. I should be glad if you will share that lunch with me, either here or in the Cabbage White in Newtown Square.'

'I don't drink.' In the face of Kemp's studied politeness, and indeed friendliness, Dempster was finding it hard to remain surly. 'But I could do with a bite to eat. Got no breakfast. Wanted to have it out with you.'

'Right. I'll get some sandwiches brought in. Coffee or tea?'

Discussion of their meal was short, then Kemp showed his visitor where the washroom was, and on Dempster's return handed him the morning paper and asked him to make himself comfortable while he himself signed some letters. He knew the local delicatessen wouldn't be long in providing their lunch, and the food was tolerable if unexciting.

In fact Daniel Dempster ate it greedily, and had two large mugs of tea – something the staff at Gillorns excelled in making.

Under Kemp's gentle, but persistent, questioning, he spoke of his friendship with Roger Warrender, and made no secret of the fact that they had first met whilst cruising in the bars of the West End. They had known each other for the last three or four years, but, as Daniel explained, his job as first mate on a cargo ship travelling the world meant long periods when they did not see one another at all. It was clear, however, that this state of affairs had been about to end.

'My old dad died in the summer and left me the house in Edmonton. And a bit of money. I was for giving up the sea. I'd done my whack. I'd paid into a good pension.' Kemp had some difficulty in putting a name to the man's accent; certainly from the North, either Scotland or Ulster, with its short 'a's and the occasional glottal stop, but like many men who'd seen all the ports of the seven seas Dempster's voice could change easily from a gutteral growl to a perfectly clear, clipped English.

'It was the state Roger had got himself into. That decided me. He needed looking after, the poor sod . . . And I could have done it, better than most. As I've told you, I don't drink. As to drugs, I've seen the lot, from Mexico to the Baltic. It's a fool's game . . ., But I learned about treatments, too, Mr Kemp, and I'd have done good by Roger . . .'

'How long have you been ashore this time, Mr Dempster?'

'We docked three weeks ago. I spent time at the firm's offices talking with the bosses as to my pension rights, and what notice I'd be giving them. Wanted that all fixed before I told Roger. Couldn't get through to him on the phone. Some sassy female always saying he's too ill to see people . . . Don't understand it. He'd always see me. I'd got it all planned, right?'

'So you never did get to see him?

Daniel shook his head. He made no attempt to hide his emotion. He took out a large, very clean handkerchief and wiped his eyes. 'This last was a long trip,' he said, 'South America and the Canaries. Last time I saw Roger was in the early summer. Even then I was worried. He looked terrible. I'd rather not have left him, but I'd already signed on for that voyage. When I'd been on shore leave I'd seen him every day. We were closer than we'd ever been. That's why I wanted it to be permanent. He needed looking after by me . . . All that rehab stuff was nonsense. Soon's he's out of those places he's back on the bottle, or the powders. He needed to have someone there . . . And not that starchy creature Dr Aumary got for him.'

Kemp nearly said 'the ubiquitous Miss Maitland' but refrained; Daniel Dempster was worthy of more than snide comment. Instead, he observed that he had met the nurse-housekeeper installed at the Crownberry Avenue flat, and he gathered that Daniel had met her as well.

'She was at the funeral. And she seemed to be in charge of the arrangements when we went back to Roger's flat.' He thought for a moment, and then shook his head, mournfully. 'I shouldn't have gone on that last trip. I should have stayed with Roger. He had got so much worse in his habits. The drug addiction was taking its toll of his health. But he assured me his brother-in-law would put him to rights and, him being a doctor, I didn't doubt it. All he told me was that Dr Aumary had got him a housekeeper. I didn't know she was a nurse as well. She was very hostile to me, Mr Kemp. She stopped me seeing Roger.'

Kemp could well imagine it: Millicent Maitland was the dragon at the door of the cave, and he could guess her attitude to a man like Dempster. What in Roger Warrender she might forgive as weakness, because he was 'family', she would have no time for in others.

Dempster seemed to be following his line of thought for he said: 'She was out to break up our friendship. I could see that.'

'And Dr Aumary, you'd met him before?'

'Yes, when he was over from America he'd call to see Roger, and seemed friendly enough to me. Spoke to me afterwards about Roger's health, and the treatment he'd recommended. Asked me for Roger's comments, and what was said between us . . .' Dempster stopped, and seemed to look at his words as if seeing the situation in a new light.

'Like a spy?' Kemp asked.

Dempster looked shocked for a moment. 'Well, he was the only relative taking an interest. He seemed to have genuine sympathy, and of course to me he was the doctor. I just hoped he'd do Roger some good but all he was suggesting was more and more rehab. That wasn't the right way for Roger. And then this Maitland person who seemed to be trying to keep me from him . . . I tend to trust people, Mr Kemp, but now I've got to thinking . . .' His voice trailed off, as he got on with thoughts which were taking him down another road.

Kemp realized that the man's initial feelings of rage towards himself, pointed by both the Aumarys, were wearing off, while real grief settled in.

'Did Roger ever mention someone with the name Perce Cavendish?' Kemp asked.

119

'No. We'd made a kind of agreement never to talk about our pasts. Does no good, that . . . Raking out the ashes of dead fires. I knew he was a toff from the first but I wasn't after his money. He was getting through it pretty quickly, anyhow.'

'What do you suppose set him off drinking in the first place?' Kemp was genuinely interested. Although he had his own ideas on the subject he would like to hear Dempster's opinion.

The other man took time to answer. This was no snap judgement – a lot of ponderous thought had gone into it. 'He'd never worked, never had to. Work's what makes a man, work and an aim in life. Roger had none. That family of his, owned land, didn't they? Sold off in dribs and drabs, bit of money here, bit of money there, never enough for Roger. Must have been clever once, him being up at Oxford, but he'd not the stamina to keep a job . . .' Kemp noticed that Roger Warrender seemed to have continued his mother's notion that 'being up at Oxford' could only have one meaning. He himself had wondered if in the business college he was actually in, Roger had ever got beyond double-entry bookkeeping.

Daniel was shaking his head, sadly. 'He was like a piece of driftwood when I met him. Going nowhere. The drink got to him, then it was the drugs, he just didn't care. Then he got really ill when his brother-in-law was over from the States the first time. The doctor was shocked how bad he'd got. He started him on the rehab and the detox programmes, but Roger just slid out from under. Got depressed, and then he'd talk a bit about the family. Told me his dad was a failure in the City, so he'd not even try. Kept saying, "There's no place for me, Dan . . ." That's how he felt; as if there was no place for him. So he drank to escape, and then got into drugs . . . That thing about his father, it rankled, said it ruined his life. That's no attitude, Mr Kemp, a man's got to work for himself, he's got to have an aim. I'm talking too much . . .'

'Indeed you are not, Mr Dempster. You're talking a lot of sense. I think you were Roger's one good friend . . .'

'That Dr Aumary, now he'd ask me about Roger when he got me alone, asked me just like you, did he talk about the past, when he was under the influence. I told him we'd agreed neither of us would talk about the past, and anyway when I was around I saw to it that Roger didn't drink.' Again he shook his head from side to side. 'I wasn't there enough. I didn't give him the time I should. Do you know, Mr Kemp, when I made up my mind to leave the sea I thought about training as a counsellor, drug abuse and alcoholics. I got leaflets about it.' His face was quite red by now, as if ashamed of what he was saying. 'I never told nobody that, not till now.'

'It does you credit, Daniel – may I call you that? I think Roger Warrender was fortunate in having met you. I'm only sorry . . .' He stopped, for the man had his handkerchief out again, and was mopping at his eyes.

'I was too damned late. And that bitch kept me away, deliberately . . .'

Some of Dempster's truculence was returning. It was a more hopeful sign, and Kemp took advantage of it.

'Which brings us back to the bottle of whisky. It's a wonder they didn't blame you for bringing it in.'

Dempster stared at him, angry. 'What the hell? I never got near the place . . . As for the whisky, it would be like handing him poison. That Maitland woman, did she ever tell Roger that I'd rung? Do you really think she'd do a thing like that?'

'I've no doubt of it. She has a habit of ignoring unwelcome phone calls. But don't worry, Mr Dempster, I'm not letting the matter rest. I'm working on it. By the way, were you told that Roger had already attempted suicide once before?'

'Dr Aumary said something about it. I didn't believe him. But if he was as ill as they say . . . I dunno. I'm not thinking straight. Roger would say from time to time he'd no use for living . . . But, suicide . . . That wasn't like him. He'd get so low, then he'd crack a joke, and it'ud be all right again. Leastways, that's what he was like a year or two ago, but if he got really ill . . .' Dempster was getting to his feet.

'Perhaps we shall never know,' Kemp said, quietly. 'What will you do now?'

'Go back to sea. Tell the bosses I've had a rethink . . .' The melancholy brown eyes looked into a future of grey seascapes, and no landfall . . .

'Give me your present whereabouts,' said Kemp. 'You've no address on your card.'

'No need for it while I was aboard ship. I'm at my own place in Edmonton: 22 Balaclava Crescent. I'll be there till I sign on for another voyage.' The long sigh he gave seemed to come right up from his shiny boots.

Kemp held out his hand. 'I'm very glad to have met you, Mr Dempster. I'll be in touch before you sail again.'

As Dempster was making for the door, his stride less purposeful than when he came in, Kemp was struck by a thought. 'By the way,' he said, 'when did you first know that Roger had died?'

'I spoke with the shipping company last Tuesday morning, then I went over to Crownberry Avenue in the afternoon. There was that Maitland woman there, and Roger's sister, who told me. I asked about a funeral, she was a bit reluctant to tell me but her husband butts in and says it's OK. He knew me, of course. She didn't. Odd that it was the brother-in-law who cared.'

'He was Roger's cousin, too.'

'Well, well, I never knew that. But, then, we didn't talk families much . . .'

'I suppose there weren't many at the funeral?'

122

'More undertakers than folk,' said Daniel, gruffly.

'"We buried him quietly . . ."' Kemp murmured to himself.

'He was cremated,' said Dempster, who had sharp ears, and no head for poetry. He was looking at the splintered hinge of the door, and turned back.

'I'd like to . . .'

But Kemp waved a hand to avoid what he saw as the inevitable offer to pay, or Dempster was the kind of man who would have picked up a new door-frame from somewhere, and put it up himself within hours.

'Don't worry, the insurance will take care of all that. As I said, I'll be in touch. That's a promise.'

Sixteen

Detective Sergeant Martin was in the CID room at Newtown Police Station when he was told that Lennox Kemp wanted a word with him. Martin, who had hopes of promotion, sighed; pay-back time, he thought, I wonder what he wants out of me?

He was very relieved to find it was nothing recent. 'But that must be a very old file, Mr Kemp – going back twenty years.'

'I know it is but I still want it. And I think your Chief Inspector West would have no hesitation – if he was here.'

'I don't know.' DS Tony Martin hesitated. Would it be wrong to get someone to rummage through old records just to get out an old file for a local solicitor, or would it be even more wrong to risk upsetting his Inspector by being obstructive? Decisions, decisions, that's what it would be all about when he himself became an Inspector. In the meantime . . . He remembered the friendship that John Upshire had had with this same solicitor, the plaudits everyone had received when their cases were solved with his aid; he himself had been part of the team highly commended for the arrest of a local killer last year – again they had been helped by the shrewdness and tenacity of Lennox Kemp. His firm, Gillorns, had an excellent criminal practice in the town and their co-operation with the local police could always be relied on – unlike others in the law who, in Tony Martin's opinion, were out to feather their own nests and clobber the police at every turn.

'I'm sorry my Chief Inspector's away at the moment – a conference up in the Midlands, but I see no reason why I shouldn't have that file produced for you. It'll take an hour or so. Of course, I can't help being curious . . .'

'Don't be, Tony. It's not part of your job to be curious except when you're on a case, and something tells me you've got nothing very big on at the moment.'

DS Martin grimaced. 'You're right, things are a bit slack, so we should be pleased. OK, I'll have a look for that file myself, and give you a ring.'

Kemp left the police station in better spirits than he'd been in the morning. Before the visit of Daniel Dempster he had been sitting back, waiting for things to happen, now he'd decided to make things happen for himself. That was what had taken him to the local station at two in the afternoon; he would have that file by the evening.

He took it home and devoured it. At least that's what his wife said later.

'You went at it with your teeth,' she said, 'like a cannibal . . .'

He handed it to her, and asked her to have a read of it, and then they would discuss it. In the meantime he wanted to think.

It was at their favourite time, after dinner over coffee in the sitting room, Elspeth safely asleep, when she gave it back.

'A bit thin,' she said, 'there's not a lot to it.'

'Well, there wouldn't be, with the chief protagonist dead before all the evidence against him was substantiated. The case was left in limbo . . .'

Mary reflected. 'It would have been different if he'd had someone, a relative or maybe a friend who might have thought his name might be cleared, or who might have at least tried to give his side of the story. Here we've got nothing.'

'What do you think of the statements?'

'Well, there's not many, for a start, considering the publicity the original disappearance got in the press, and on television. Of course, there's the usual cranks.'

'John Upshire saw those off pretty quickly. I think he handled the case well, what there was of it, though he didn't follow possible paths.'

'I know the one you're interested in. But his men couldn't have questioned Dr Ayres immediately after Perce Cavendish made his statement, she was away on a cruise holiday. And that's in her diary.'

'So's the altered date that made me suspicious in the first place. Look at it.'

This time, Mary made a more careful scrutiny of the page. There was no doubt an effort had been made to change an entry. 'An expert could make something of it,' she allowed. 'What you're trying to say is that Perce was right when he said he'd kept an appointment at Dr Ayre's surgery that afternoon, Monday the 13th of August, but the doctor herself changed her own entry later so that it looked as if she was out checking up on her over-eighties at the time he claimed he was there.'

'It's only an idea. But it was all Cavendish had when they arrested him – he gave it as his alibi. Upshire and his men were a bit dilatory in going to see Dr Enid, they left it twenty-four hours, and by then she'd left on holiday. It was three weeks before she returned to Newtown . . .'

'And by then Cavendish was in the prison hospital, and cancer had been diagnosed by the doctor there. I think the first thing he would have done – and which was nothing to do with the police – was to contact Cavendish's GP.'

'That date in the doctor's diary is so vital to the case,' said Kemp. 'Particularly when Cavendish says he had an appointment at two thirty on that afternoon. His explanation is that he was a private patient of the doctor's, and she often saw such patients in the afternoon, they didn't go at normal surgery times. When Dr Ayre eventually made a statement to the police she said this was the case, but she wasn't seeing any patients that afternoon; she was out visiting her over-eighties. She also said she hadn't seen Mr Cavendish for a few months, although she did admit he was a private patient of hers.'

'Now I've read what other people said, I see your point. The times are important. Rickie's mother saw him playing in the garden at two o'clock, what does Granny Wheatcroft say?'

Both the Kemps agreed that Mrs Wheatcroft's statement was nothing like her. It was short, giving no evidence that she might have been a talkative person, and couched in terms which could only have been used by social workers or police. She had seen the little boy in his garden when she set out from Sycamore Cottage at about half-past two o'clock. Yes, she knew him, and yes, he had acknowledged that he had seen her. There was no mention of the sun on his hair, nor that he had the face of an angel.

The statement of Mrs Amy Fenwick showed it had been taken when she was in deep distress, and sympathy and kindness showed in the manner her words were taken down, but it still amounted to a simple, cold narration of events and times. She had been baking in the kitchen most of the afternoon, she had prepared tea for them both, and gone into the garden at about four o'clock to call him. He was not there, and she never saw him again.

Although it was never suggested outright, the police had had to think originally of other reasons for the little boy's absence from the garden, but such questioning had been handled with delicacy – Kemp saw John Upshire's steady presence in this; he could be a heavyweight where criminals were concerned, but he had an innate decency towards those bewildered and distraught, particularly in the early stages of a case. It became apparent that Dominic had been an obedient little boy, and if told to stay in the garden he would have done so. That afternoon he should have had his friend Jimmy Fletcher to play with, but Jimmy had to go to the dentist, so Dominic was alone. This too was normal: he often played alone, making up games for himself, and 'play-acting' – one of his favourite pastimes, and the one which had brought him to the notice of Percival Cavendish.

Mrs Vera Morris, the head teacher at Oldgreen Primary School said that Dominic Fenwick was one of her most able pupils, ahead of his age in reading, and well-behaved. It was for these reasons, and for his acting skills, that he had been chosen for the part of Puck in the little playlet based on *A Midsummer Night's Dream*, which the children had performed in July on the Common.

The curate of Ember Church also spoke glowingly of the little boy who had just begun to attend Sunday school along with other children from his neighbourhood. The Reverend Barnes said Dominic had stood up manfully to the other tragedy in his young life: when his father, Edward Fenwick, a soldier in the Midshires, had lost his life in the Falklands.

Mary, who had been reading some of the statements aloud, stopped and stared at her husband when she reached this point.

'I know,' he said, grimly. 'When I read that I wondered how Perce Cavendish escaped lynching long before he was taken into custody . . . Amy Fenwick was a war widow, they only came to live at Fernley Cottage through the Army Benevolent Fund, who paid the rent. Edward Fenwick was in the regular Army.'

'The only child of his mother, and she a widow,' murmured Mary. 'Oh, Lennox . . .'

'The papers made much of it,' said Kemp, gruffly. 'I spent the rest of this afternoon at the offices of the *Newtown Gazette*,' he went on, in explanation, 'and they filled in what's not on that file. They'd a good reporter,

Dave Cormac. I don't think he missed anything and he was still at it when the nationals gave up. Of course everything was sub judice when Cavendish was arrested, but there was another spurt of interest when he died. Cormac tried to get an interview with Mrs Fenwick, then living with her parents in London, but he was promptly seen off by her parents.'

Mary nodded. 'Quite right, too. "How do you feel, Amy, now the killer of your child is dead?" How callous can you get?'

'Don't blame Cormac, he was only doing his job. And the press in this country is no worse than in yours.'

His wife ignored the dig, and got on with her reading.

'What a lot of people said they saw a red van that day once they knew it was a suspect vehicle. Even Granny Wheatcroft comes up with seeing it in the lanes that afternoon.'

'I've a shrewd suspicion that was after the police were on to Perce Cavendish, and everyone knew it was a red van he used to drive around in.'

'They pulled him in for questioning within a few days of the body being found. Why were they so fast? There seems to be a gap in the record once they had a murder scene, as they call it.'

'That's one of the questions I'm going to ask John Upshire when I see him, but I think it was one of his old mates in the Met who put them on to Perce Cavendish. And Jim Sutherland said something to me about him having had accusations already of sexual assaults on children.'

'You mean convictions?' Mary had glanced up, sharply.

Kemp shook his head. 'No, or they would be in that file. But it looks to me as if the police had suspicions when his name cropped up. Once he was dead, of course, people could say what they like about him – and obviously did.'

Mary was almost at the end of turning over pages. 'Oh,'

she exclaimed, 'they found Rickie's trainers hidden in that van of his. How awful! How could he possibly . . .?'

'Perhaps he hadn't time to get rid of them . . . Perhaps he'd forgotten. All Cavendish says in his own statement is that he didn't know they were there, he's almost inferring that they were planted . . .'

'By the police? Surely that was a foolish attitude?'

'It would be when John Upshire was in charge. There are a lot of questions I want to ask him when he gets back from this wee holiday of his, and one of them is why they were so quickly off the mark where Cavendish was concerned. They searched that van of his within a day of the body being found.'

'They did search other vehicles as well,' said Mary, trying to be fair. She handed the folder back to her husband.

'I think I've read enough,' she said. 'So, it's a sad story, but at least it has an end – or closure, as they're beginning to call it. Perhaps it was by God's will that some kind of justice was meted out to Perce Cavendish for what he did.'

'But what if he didn't do it?' Kemp asked a merely rhetorical question; he did not share his wife's view that the Almighty could be left to shoulder the responsibility when justice on earth had failed.

Seventeen

Even cars have to have appointments made for them these days, thought Kemp the next morning as he drove his ten-year-old Rover into David Lorimer's garage on the ring road. He'd come early, however, because he wanted a word with the proprietor, who was an old friend.

Naturally David gave him coffee in the comfortable show-room with its leather furniture and enticing brochures. 'You won't get me that way,' said Kemp, appreciating the thought. 'I'll hang on to this one for a year or two yet.'

'I could get you one straight from Longbridge, dealer's discount . . . No, I thought not. Cars aren't your thing, are they, Lennox?'

'Which is why I let you look after them for me. At least you look prosperous enough out here. A long way from your first effort at the Tollcross twenty years ago.'

'Don't remind me.' Looking back, David Lorimer had to acknowledge it had been a bad time for him. The Development Corporation in their wisdom had chosen a route for the new ring road which bypassed his garage at Tollcross, effectively cutting him off from his livelihood. Fortunately, but only after a struggle, he had received compensation enough to buy his present premises, which, as Kemp remarked, had flourished.

'It was you I have to thank,' he said now to his visitor, 'you guided me through that mishmash of planning law the Development people set up just to strangle folk like me. If

131

I can't sell you a car what can I do for you – you didn't get here early to bribe me over an MOT certificate.'

'No. I wanted to ask you if you remember a man called Perce Cavendish who was in Newtown twenty years ago.'

'Of course I remember Cavendish. He killed the little Fenwick boy. Frightful thing. Then Cavendish himself died. I knew him quite well when I was out at the old garage because he'd lodgings near there and he'd bring in his van from time to time. Like you he'd no idea what went on under the bonnet of any vehicle. Oddly enough, I quite liked Cavendish before it happened. Easygoing kind of chap, a bit airy-fairy but seemed decent enough.'

'He brought his van in to you? Was that the red one?

Lorimer nodded. 'Yes, that was the one, an old Post Office van. You could buy them fairly cheap at the time. His was a bit of a rust-bucket because he'd neglected it, but the engine was all right. I remember him bringing it in for a respray and saying he didn't care what colour it was as long as it could go on the road. I gave him the cheapest paint job I could, a horrible darkish brown but he said it was OK – it would hide the rust . . .'

'Any idea when that was?' asked Kemp, hopefully.

'First week in August 1979,' Lorimer replied, promptly.

'How on earth do you remember the date, David? It's over twenty years.'

'Ah, but I'd every reason to remember that week because it loomed over me all that summer. It was the week the Development Corporation and Newtown Council were getting together to decide the new route for the ring road. How could I forget that week – I never slept a wink any night of it. The meeting was on the ninth of August, and of course there was all that secrecy and the final route wasn't in fact chosen till the following month, but I didn't know that at the time. But I do remember Perce Cavendish bringing in his van for the respray that week, and me thinking that I might soon end up like him, driving a beat-up old vehicle, with no job and no money. Why is it one always thinks the worst at four o'clock in the morning?'

'Happens to all of us,' said Kemp, who had been through it himself. 'But you're saying that although Cavendish had a red van in July, it was dark brown by August.'

'That's it. Nasty colour, really but he didn't mind.'

'But lots of people were saying they saw his red van about the time the little boy went missing,' Kemp persisted.

Lorimer shrugged. 'Well, you know what people are like. There were plenty round here at the time who said I was bankrupt.'

Kemp got to his feet. 'Thanks for the coffee, David. I hope my old Rover gets its MOT certificate again this year, I'd hate to have to fork out for one of your lovely new ones. Hard times, you know.'

David Lorimer roared with laughter. 'The day you lawyers fall on hard times will be the day my cars start talking to each other. Pick it up this evening or you can have it by lunchtime if you like.'

'Six o'clock will do. We lawyers have to work, you know.'

'Want a lift into the town? One of my men can drive you.'

'No, thanks, I'll get a bus,' said Kemp, primly. 'I want no favours. Just pass my bloody Rover . . .'

He was pleased to find when he collected it at closing time that it had indeed passed its crucial test, and was safe to go about the high roads and byways of the country for another year.

He was not pleased on reaching home to be told that Lettice Aumary had phoned.

'Would be glad if you'd ring her at the Crownberry flat,' Mary reported in imitation upper-crust English.

'Is she still hostile?' asked her husband, anxiously. 'I'll not have her being rude to you.'

133

'Oh, her sort are never rude. Just cold and very distant, like snow on a mountain.'

'Perhaps she wants to apologize. It was all some frightful mistake, Miss Maitland had been left out in the sun too long, and they're all so sorry for what was said.'

Mary grinned, but she had to tell him there had been no hint of a climbdown in Mrs Aumary's voice. 'She spoke to me in the way she probably does to the maid in her New York apartment – coloured, of course.'

'Well, she can wait,' said Kemp, decisively, 'while I bath my daughter and have supper. I'm not altering my domestic schedule this evening for any of the Warrender clan.'

'Good. I'm glad to see you're getting unstuck from that old feeling. For a while I began to fear it was permanent. Here, you take this one, she's getting too giggly.' Mary unwound the child's arms from her neck, and handed her over to Lennox, who had been wriggling his ears at her from behind her mother's back.

It was after nine when he finally dialled the number he'd been given by the late Roger Warrender. It was still on the scrap of paper knocking about on the writing desk; if things were going to go on like this he might have to put it in the book. He hoped they weren't; he'd had enough of Lettice and her spurts of anger.

When she answered she was obviously in the middle of one of them for her voice came high and sharp: 'Why have you taken so long to ring me back? Mary said you'd be in just after six.'

'I've been in the bath with Elspeth.' As a conversation-stopper, it worked. All he heard was an indrawn breath. He relented, and went on: 'My daughter, you know . . .' He wasn't sure whether it was fair to use the child in what seemed to be a war of words with Lettice, but he couldn't think of anything else to say. He tried to keep his voice friendly when he asked what she wanted.

She was still complaining. 'I expected you to ring immediately, Lennox. Now it'll be too late for me to return to the hotel, and I will have to stay the night here.'

'Why can't Tod drive you back to London?'

'Tod's up in Edinburgh. I've been left to clear up Roger's things . . . It's heart-breaking, Lennox, being in the flat . . .' Her voice softened for a moment, and he could almost believe that she had feelings after all.

'I'm so sorry, Lettice.'

'And that's why I'm phoning you. I can't let things stay as they are.'

'You mean you've come to your senses about my visit to your brother?

'I mean no such thing. All I want to know is why you should do such a thing. I've really tried hard, Lennox, to give you the benefit of the doubt, because in the past I always trusted you. I still can't understand why you did it.'

'Did what?

'Take that bottle of whisky in to Roger. I know you were probably drunk at the time, but even so.'

Kemp could feel his anger rising. 'You know nothing, Lettice. You were not there, and somehow you and your husband have swallowed this incredible story told to you by someone who is either embittered or deranged.'

'Don't you say a word against Miss Maitland! After all she has been through, after all she did for my poor brother . . .'

There is something quite unsatisfactory about telephone quarrels: neither of the antagonists can see the other's expression, so cannot register a hit, neither can watch for signs of surrender or defeat, and if either of them eventually resorts to physical violence all they'll smash is the rented property of the phone company. Keeping quiet for a few seconds, and thinking along these lines, Kemp managed

to calm down, and say, evenly: 'I'm going to ring off,
Lettice. Unless you have something constructive to say, this
is the end of our conversation.'

He hoped his tone sounded wise and judicial, like a judge
at the end of a long day. It seemed to work.

'It's just that I can't leave things as they are.' Her voice
was lower now, and more hesitant, as if she was no longer
so sure of herself. 'If we could meet and talk.'

'I don't see that it would help unless . . . But, perhaps
you're right, Lettice. I've no wish to lose your friendship,
a friendship I once valued highly . . .'

His words had an immediate effect. 'Oh, we must meet.
Yes, that would be the thing. I simply can't go back to the
States without seeing you again, getting some kind of expla-
nation . . .'

'Whoa, there. You're running on too fast. When do you
and Tod go back?'

'We only have another week. Could you come to the flat
tomorrow?

'No way. Nor the next day. We'll have to leave it till the
weekend, and I'm only coming, Lettice, because you'll be
upset if I don't.' He wanted to be certain who was going
to be in the driving-seat.

'Tod won't be back until Saturday. Could you come on
Friday evening? It would be better if we met alone.' She
sounded like a young woman arranging a clandestine date.

'I'll be there about eight. No food necessary. Oh, and
send Miss Maitland out to the pictures.'

He had the satisfaction of hearing what could be a muffled
laugh, or a stifled gasp, and then a very small 'yes', so that
he was assured of the time and place of the assignation –
the fancy word seemed to go with the tricksy ways of Lettice
Aumary.

He turned to meet the calm, enquiring gaze of his wife.
'Well,' she said, 'I heard all that from your end, and very

peculiar it sounded. What's the Honourable Lettuce Leaf up to now?'

'I wish I knew.'

'But you're going to meet her? Does the husband know?'

'Not from the way she was careful to make it a night when he was away from home. Isn't that usual in these circumstances?'

'I've no idea what circumstances these are. Seriously, Lennox, I don't like any of this. I'm not sure I want you to go to that flat again – and on a Friday, too. Look what happened to you that other Friday . . .'

'I had marked the coincidence. And, no, she's still repeating their stupid accusation. I think, perhaps, that's the reason I agreed to go.' Indeed, he had surprised himself but, on reflection, he was still curious to find out why the story had been concocted in the first place, and where the prissy Miss Maitland came in. Like Lettice herself, he could not let the matter rest until he'd found out more. If the Aumarys left for America without explanation he might never know.

He sat down and took up the evening paper, but his thoughts were elsewhere and kept coming back to that Friday afternoon, the rain-swept porch, and his own odd appearance. He had gone over it in his mind so many times that confusion had arisen between what he actually remembered, and what had actually happened. He had recently read an article about the 'sins' of memory; how experience is wiped away as it occurs, and when one recollects the event it is more of a reconstruction than a literal replay. There is always an element of forgetfulness, an editing and a selection no matter how objective one tries to be.

He had been amazed, for instance, how many times since that day he had seen in his mind's eye a bottle of Teacher's whisky. Of course he must have seen one of these perhaps a hundred times in the past, and even occasionally bought one, but he had not been prepared for the strong image of such a bottle which now rose in his mind when he attempted to relive the happenings of that afternoon. Now he saw the bottle – the familiar golden hue of the liquid, the fawn label with the black lines and the name writ large – and he saw it in the surroundings of the very wineshop in London where he had purchased the single malt for Dinah's father. Had he seen it that particular day, or was it just because it was such a familiar brand that it now figured so largely in his mind?

Although the very idea was ludicrous, he'd even wondered whether he'd in fact bought such a bottle in that shop that day. This thought had occurred to him when he'd recently awoken from a bad dream in which he was surrounded by serried ranks of whisky bottles, and had unerringly picked out a Teacher's. It took some painstaking reconstruction in his mind to dismiss this as a depressing phantasy, yet the thought lingered . . .

Mary watched him staring at the football page and, knowing he was never a great fan of the game, she decided that action was necessary.

'Shall I give Brenda a ring? They might have come back from holiday by now.'

Kemp roused himself. 'If they have, then I'd better explain to John about that file before Sergeant Martin does. John still has a habit of wandering into the Station from time to time, he says it's for a chat with his old pal Inspector West, but it's really because he likes to smell the dust.'

The Upshires had just returned, and Brenda was unpacking. 'Yes, lovely time, great hotel. John? Well, you know what's he's like, not the one for hotel life . . .'

'What about coming to supper tomorrow night? You can tell me all about the Torquay shops, and John can complain to Lennox about the over-sixties.'

'That would be great because I've got nothing in to eat, and after all the lovely food we had I'd be stumped for a meal. Usual time, Mary?'

'Yes, eightish . . . Hold on, Brenda, Lennox would like a word with John.'

John Upshire was rather grumpy when told about the murder file. 'Can't think what you wanted it for. Case long dead and buried. But, knowing you, one can't be sure of anything, eh? I suppose you want to talk about it?'

No beating about the bush with ex-Superintendent Upshire. 'I'm afraid so, John. But, never mind that, Mary'll give you a good dinner, though maybe not up to the standard of those high-class hotels you and Brenda frequent now you've retired . . .'

'You can have them,' Upshire growled. 'Me, I'm just glad to be home where I can put my feet up. See you tomorrow night.'

'Feeling better now?' asked Mary as her husband put down the phone. 'You've got something to look forward to. You and John can retire to the study after dinner with that precious file, while Brenda and I do the washing-up.'

'I don't know why I bought you a dishwasher,' complained Kemp, mildly. 'You seem to prefer getting your hands in the sink.'

'Just as you prefer getting your paws into the dirt of old cases instead of concentrating on present business,' retorted Mary.

She had a point, so next day Kemp worked exceptionally hard on his clients' affairs, had a working lunch with his colleagues, and by the middle of the afternoon felt free of any left-over guilt from her remark.

He had business at Ember but he took the back roads by way of Fernley Common, and stopped his car on the lane above the two cottages, Sycamore and Fernley, the one so neat and tidy, the other so neglected, its garden overgrown by nettles, its flower beds and lawns invisible under their persistent strength.

He walked up the path towards the Common, surprised

at its steepness, and his own shortness of breath. He stopped
where the tracks converged by the signpost to Ember. It
would have been here that Alice Wheatcroft would have
looked back down on her own cottage and the one across
the lane. Here was where the Common proper began, and
it was quite high; below, the roofs showed their colours to
the sun, the Wheatcroft's slatey-blue, the now-abandoned
Fernley yellow and russet where lichen had spread along
the tiles.

Kemp continued to look down. It was very quiet. In the
lanes the brambles were finished, and the berry-gatherers
had long gone. The wind buzzed gently through the dry
leaves on the hawthorn hedgerows; otherwise all was still.
Beneath him the hedges marked out where the various lanes
ran along the edge of the common land, but the little roads
themselves were obscured.

And it had been the height of summer then, he told
himself, the hedges would have been higher and thicker.
You could not have seen a car on any of these lanes from
here. He remembered Mrs Wheatcroft's words because they
had been important to him and he had questioned her carefully. 'Back down on the roofs of the cottages the sun it
were so bright you could hardly see.' That would have been
quite accurate that day with the sun at its highest, even
today in the autumn light the roofs were indeed catching
what there was of sunshine. Then she had gone on: 'And
there's that flash of red between the hedges . . .' When he
had asked her where, she had replied, instantly, with no
doubt in her voice: 'Why, along the lane between ours and
Fernley . . .'

But Mrs Wheatcroft's statement in the police file was
different. Was it suggested to her that she'd seen a red van?
'They called it a vehicle,' she'd said – it certainly hadn't
come from her. It was only after Cavendish had been
arrested that she went along with everybody else in thinking,

and saying that it was indeed the van driven by Cavendish which they all knew was red.

Except that in August, it wasn't.

Kemp went back to his car. It was easier going down and in a little while he was on the main road to Ember. What had been quite a walk for Alice to her friend's house in the village was only a matter of minutes in a car. His mind kept coming back to the vehicle that was seen that day; it turned up in so many statements – surely there must have been plenty of other vehicles about, there was little mention of them. Something he would raise with John Upshire later, if indeed the ex-Inspector was in the mood to answer such queries. He hadn't liked the case being talked about when Kemp had revived it by mentioning the diaries which had belonged to Dr Ayre; tact and diplomacy would be required tonight as well as Mary's good cooking.

Eighteen

'I like this room,' said John Upshire, putting his feet up in a recliner chair in what the Kemps termed their study, 'though I wouldn't do much studying in it.'

The house at 2 Albert Crescent had been a Victorian mansion when it was built, with a back garden leading down to what was then a sweet stretch of the River Lea, willow trees and all. Sadly, industry had taken its toll on this pleasant aspect just as the house had suffered depredation from a wartime bomb, and the interior had had to be remodelled several times to keep the electricity cables and the plumbing up to date. Now it was a comfortable enough residence but lacked any aesthetic value or architectural worth. Both the Kemps loved it for its high ceilings, and long windows which seemed to let in the sky, and for its air of having survived the worst the years could throw at it.

Kemp looked round the small, square room which led, surprisingly, off the dining room but in the opposite direction from the kitchen. 'I think it must have originally been something to do with the butler, or where the maids sat around waiting to be called, or perhaps it was just where the master of the house could retire with his cigar after dinner.'

'Wise man,' said John. 'I could do with a place like it – not that I smoke nowadays, but just somewhere to sit back and do nothing . . . A brandy? A good idea, Lennox. Brenda is driving tonight, the woman has her uses . . .'

'Now, now, John, you know you like being looked after.'
He put down their two glasses on the table between them,
and went over to his desk for the file.

'You've been softening me up all evening for this.'
Upshire sighed. 'I've been thinking it over since you brought
it up first, the Fenwick murder, and perhaps, yes, I don't
mind going through it again. Why should I worry now about
things that weren't mebbe done straight, and things that
didn't work out as they should have done. It's all past
history, anyway.'

John Upshire's changed attitude made the ensuing discussion easier than Kemp had feared. They went through the
file as it stood, paying particular attention to certain of the
statements, Kemp marking in his own mind the omissions
and gaps he had noticed in his own reading of them.

'The way we got on to Cavendish was simple, the way
we did things in those days before we had computers and
central information networks,' explained Upshire. 'We had
our own network. We talked more between colleagues at
other stations, everything was more open in our enquiries
about known criminals – aye, and them not so known, like
any suspicious characters who'd crossed our paths. And that
brought in the sexual lot – from occasional flashers to real
paedophiles like Cavendish.'

'I saw the note in the file that was passed on from one
of your mates in the Met. Sergeant Mottram, was that it?'

'Billy Mottram, that's right. I'd worked with him when
I was up in the City. He'd come across Cavendish in a case
that never got to court, and there were young boys involved.
The Vice Squad were suspicious of a place off Drury Lane.
There were theatre names got mentioned, big names.
Anyway, that one never got off the ground, but Billy
Mottram had kept tabs on our Perce, and knew he'd gone
to live in Newtown, so when he heard about the murder of
the young lad Billy gives me a bell. And don't be looking

at me like that, Lennox, there were other chaps in the Met who'd been on the watch for Cavendish over the years. We'd every reason to bring him in.'

'You got off to a good start when you searched his van. Why on earth did the man keep the shoes in there?'

'We were too quick for him. And it weren't only the shoes. There were traces of Dominic all over the place. We didn't have the experts with their DNA testing that we have now, but we had enough. There were fibres from his T-shirt, blond hairs from his head, all sticking to the upholstery of that van.'

'Perce Cavendish says he wasn't surprised. Said Dominic had been in the van scores of times, he'd taken him to rehearsals of the play, Dominic had helped him load the scenery from the village hall.'

'But he couldn't explain the shoes. Bowled him over, that one did. It was me that did that interview. I'll never forget his face. We could have held him on those trainers alone, but there was other stuff as you can see from the file.'

'The sightings of a red van? At least four witnesses said they saw a red van near Fernley Common that afternoon, and two of them volunteered that at the time they'd thought it looked like the one that Perce Cavendish drove.'

'That's right. And before you say anything, it was never suggested to them that it was Cavendish's van.'

'Of course not,' said Kemp, keeping a neutral tone. 'But by the thirteenth of August it wasn't a red van anyway.'

'How was that?'

'Mr Cavendish had had a respray. When the boy was snatched, the van was brown.'

'That's not on the file. What was probably meant was a reddish-brown. The thing is, the trainers were found in Perce Cavendish's van – that's fact. And he couldn't deny it was his van no matter the colour.'

'Do you actually remember what colour it was?

144

'I was the Inspector in charge,' Upshire growled, 'of course I remember, it was a reddish brown. I don't see the point of all this.'

But Kemp hadn't finished. 'Simply as a matter of interest, John, were there in fact any other suspects?'

'No, there weren't. Isn't that clear from the file? There was nobody who would have harmed that boy. At first people thought it might have been a passing motorist – the usual wishful thinking, it can't be one of us. But Fernley Common's local land, no roads cross it, only lanes leading nowhere. And, of course, when the lad's body was found stuffed into that hedge we knew it had to be someone local, someone who'd had a place to keep it for two days. You see from the path report what the medics said.'

Kemp looked it up. 'That death had taken place more than forty-eight hours before, and that the body had been brought to the place where it was found within the last few hours, that is sometime on the fifteenth of August.'

'And our man Cavendish had no alibi for that day. Said he slept in that morning at his lodgings in Ember village and was home all day. Well, there weren't anyone to vouch for that. No one had seen him or his van, which he kept in an old shed at the back of the terrace house he lived in.'

'Funny that he should take such care with his first alibi, for the day the boy was taken, yet he seems to have made no attempt to try one out again.'

'Didn't expect us to get on to him so fast. He'd no satis-factory explanation as to where he'd been the day the body must have been transported across Newtown to the main road where it was found. But when we got those trainers out from under some stuff at the back of his van, well, that about clinched it anyway.'

'Why on earth would he keep them?' Kemp wondered.

'As I said, we were on to him too fast. It was then he started to blubber. I was doing the questioning at the time, and I wasn't coming heavy – not yet.' Kemp knew it was part of John Upshire's interrogative technique to act the soft-spoken sympathetic cop when that was required. 'Starts blubbing, I remember. He had to sit down. We were still in the room at his lodgings. He muttered something about the shoes being left over from one of the times Dominic had been in his van – the boy helping out with scenery and stuff for the play. But those trainers had already been shown to Amy Fenwick and they were the ones he'd been wearing in the garden that day.'

As he finished, John Upshire's eyes were wet. Kemp said nothing but was imagining the scene; there is nothing more harrowing than showing the clothes of a murdered child to his parent. He had been about to suggest the shoes could have been planted in that van by anyone, but he desisted, and changed tack.

'I see it was a farmer who first spotted the body.'

'Aye, he was going slow. Most go fast along that main road to London but he'd got a tractor on tow. Besides, farmers have a better idea of what should be in hedgerows and what shouldn't. That farmer, Trevelyn was his name as I remember, spotted the white shirt and the awkward angle, he had a look and called us.' John Upshire stopped, and was again looking back in his mind, not liking what was there.

'You know, one of the worst things was the casual way it had been thrown . . . Maybe he tried to get it over the hedge into the field, where it might have lain longer before it was found. But it had just been tossed on top of the hedge like . . . like . . . old rubbish. Unforgiveable that was . . . Had it ever come to trial . . .'

'But it didn't,' said Kemp, who was beginning to think he was leading his friend too far down an old road. 'At least finding the body put a stop to your men's search in the vicinity of Fernley and its surroundings. Reading the report, you seem to have had the whole of Newtown out searching.'

'Apart from the Force, they were all volunteers – once the fact of the disappearance got around there was no shortage of willing helpers.'

'From a wide spectrum of local society,' murmured Kemp, 'including the surviving gentry at Castleton House.'

'That would be one of the Warrenders – offered to help because he had a car and knew the countryside. I tell you, man, we took any help that was offered for my men were stretched to the limit, searching every empty building, every barn or shed, where the boy might have been hidden. At first it was hope that spurred them on, just in case he was still alive . . .'

'Nowadays the search parties would be told to be careful not to contaminate any DNA evidence . . .'

'Damn it, we were just as careful then. We listed all those taking part, and they were warned if they found anything: don't touch, stay where you are and whistle us up. We didn't need DNA to teach us that.'

'No, of course not. I was just thinking that had the murder taken place now DNA swabs from the boy and from his killer would have been conclusive of guilt. I see from the medical reports that there was no actual sexual assault despite what the press said, but there had been, as the medics put it, interference.'

'There was enough,' said Upshire, gruffly, 'to put that pervert Cavendish away for life. The lad must have screamed and that had to be stopped. So he was strangled.'

'I see from the medical report they think death must have occurred only hours after he was taken,' said Kemp, bleakly. 'I don't know whether that's a consolation or not . . .'

'Wasn't much consolation for Amy Fenwick.' John Upshire's face was savage. 'A nice woman, she was, a good woman, she was already a widow, now she's lost her

147

son . . . Her relatives took her away, thank God. Ye know what, Lennox? That crime stained the place, it was a great, ugly blot on Newtown. Even after he died . . . Cavendish, I mean . . . Folks didn't want to talk about it, as if the whole town was ashamed.'

The two men were silent while Kemp poured John another drink, which he didn't refuse.

'Do you know when Cavendish was diagnosed with having cancer? Was he in the prison hospital at the time?'

'It was out of our hands by then, but I was told by the prison doctor that he was suffering from stomach pains just after he was arrested. I don't suppose they took much notice at the time – the authorities had other things on their mind with regard to Perce Cavendish – and his health wasn't one of them. Eventually he was sent to the hospital for tests, and they said he'd had it for months.'

'That alibi of his?' Kemp was returning to the relevant pages in the file. 'It was a little while before your people went to see Dr Ayre, wasn't it?'

'She was away. A three-week cruise, as I understand it. She'd a locum in but that didn't help us. Dr Ayre wasn't the best at keeping records, anyway. Besides, it wasn't urgent, her statement could wait till she got back.'

'And it would be from the prison doctor she would hear that her patient had cancer, for he'd get in touch with Perce Cavendish's GP to find out his medical history as soon as it was diagnosed. She says just that in her statement – where she also says that she hadn't seen Cavendish for some three or four months, and in her opinion his symptoms were those of peptic ulcer, for which he was taking medication.'

'I don't know where you're going with all this, Lennox.' John Upshire was getting impatient. 'And if I were you I'd get that folder back into the Station first thing tomorrow morning before Inspector West returns from his conference.

You wouldn't want young Martin to get into trouble, now, would you?'

Kemp was indeed going to do just that; he felt that he had exhausted John on the subject of the Fernley Cottage murder, and he was risking a friendship by taking it further with him. There was still some rancour in the ex-policeman, but whether it was at the final outcome of a case which never went to trial, or a more personal dissatisfaction, it was hard to tell.

'Talking of the Warrenders,' he said now, 'the one you would know as young Roger has died recently. He'd become an alcoholic.'

'That doesn't surprise me. Too many expectations, too many mistakes. They're all the same, those so-called noble families round here – give me council house villains any day, at least you know where you are with them. I never did like the Warrenders, toffy-nosed lot they were, looking down on the town as if it was dirt – and in the end it was the town's money they were glad to take and hop it over to the States. Whatever happened to the girl, the one you were sweet on, Lennox? What was her silly name, Lettice? That was it . . .'

Fortunately for Kemp – who was in any case disinclined to answer this foolish remark – there came a bustling in the hall and a high female voice indicating that Brenda Upshire was ready to go home.

Afterwards, Mary asked him if he had got what he wanted from his old friend.

'As I didn't know what I wanted in the first place, I can't answer that. We had a discussion, and went over the file, that's all. What he said confirmed many of my own suppositions, but still left a lot of unopened envelopes.'

'You sound depressed – did it have that effect, this going over such a sad happening?'

'Perhaps . . . Sometimes I think there are no endings.

Americans, and psychoanalysts, keep talking about achieving closure as if you could go on closing cupboard doors on every experience. Events don't take place in a vacuum, they spill out, overflow, the moment can't hold them. They go rippling away into other people's lives – people who weren't even there.'

Mary looked at him with wide, serious, grey eyes. 'It wasn't only John then who was at the brandy tonight, but even allowing for that you're trying to say something profound.'

'Am I? I seem to have been left with this terrible sense of despair – it's almost palpable as if one had come up against a door leading into a desolate garden where there's no hope . . .'

'Hey, it's supposed to be the Irish who hear the howling of the banshees, not you stolid English.' She stopped, suddenly, and said, more softly, 'What is it, darling? I too can get a shiver just thinking of Amy Fenwick, who was robbed of her son . . . Or is it the man Perce Cavendish who worries you? Is it that it was all unfinished?'

Kemp nodded. 'Yes, that is what troubles me. To bring it back to basics – and I couldn't say this to John – the police did a poor job on it. Cavendish was their man from the outset, he was a hanger-on, a down-at-heel actor, and, more important from their point of view, he was homosexual. Then he dies, and they close the books. But if he didn't do it, if he wasn't guilty, then what are we left with? The event took place, the boy was killed . . .' He broke off.

'So somebody else did,' Mary finished for him.

'Perhaps that's the saddest thing of all.' Kemp began to tidy up the papers from the file. 'I'll get this folder back to the Station tomorrow. Oh, and by the way, I've been thinking over this meeting I'm supposed to be having with Lettice Warrender. The way I feel at the moment, I don't want to go. And certainly not to that flat – not on a Friday.'

'Good,' said Mary. 'Ring her up tomorrow, and tell her so. Any particular reason?'

Kemp ran his fingers through his hair. 'I simply don't know. It's just that I was thinking about it later, and even that made me depressed. I don't know whether it was just because I saw her brother there the day before he died . . . I don't know . . .'

'Unlike you to be so uncertain, Lennox. I didn't want you to go there in the first place, you know but perhaps I was only being the jealous wife.'

Kemp took her up out of her chair, and kissed her. 'Now that was silly, my darling, and you know it. Come to bed now. I'll ring Lettice in the morning.'

Nineteen

The next morning Kemp was in a disagreeable mood. His wife noticed it and said nothing; he was her man, and anyway he'd had more than his share of that brandy the night before. His staff in the office noticed it and said nothing; he was the boss, and anyway none of them had upset him.

Lettice Warrender noticed it from the tone of his voice, and sharpened her own.

'Why can't you come on Friday? You're not afraid of a couple of middle-aged women, are you, Lennox?'

Right now Kemp was feeling scared of his own shadow for no reason that he could name. Apprehension had settled on him at the very thought of waiting in that cold stone porch for the door to open . . . Remembering his distorted image in that hall mirror and seeing it through the unnerving eye of Millicent Maitland was enough to make him admit that, yes, he was afraid to meet her again.

But not Lettice, he told himself, as he thought rapidly, trying to work up some sort of believable excuse why he could not see her at the flat on Friday. Even his thinking seemed sluggish this morning, and he was too late as her imperious voice pressed on.

'Tell you what,' she was saying, 'why don't we meet on neutral ground, as it were? It would be awkward here, anyway. Miss Maitland's packing her things . . .' Did a slight note of irritability creep in there? Maybe the sacred vessel had sprung a leak.

'She's leaving?' he heard himself say, fatuously.

'Of course, she's leaving. But she's off to Australia next week, and it looks as if she brought all her worldly goods when she came to the flat.' Again, a hint of acerbity. 'So she has a lot to pack. She's thinking of taking up residence out there.'

Australia didn't sound the kind of place where one took up residence but at least it lightened his heart to know they would soon not be sharing the same space in South-East England. Again his thoughts were meandering when they should have been focused on finding an excuse.

'Are you still there?' Lettice should have remained with the Newtown Development Corporation; no shoddy builder could have withstood those icy syllables. 'Lennox? I haven't finished with you. I must know why you did it. I will not go back to the States in ignorance. What I suggest we do is meet somewhere else.'

'Where?' asked Kemp, helplessly, by now too far involved to invent any business or social reason why he should not see her on Friday night.

'What about the King's Head at those crossroads in Wanstead? Remember you once took me there after picking me up in Town?'

Why did everything she said seem to be packed with innuendo? Of course, he remembered. A desperate phone call from little Lettice Warrender out at a swinging party with some of her Benenden chums, a party that had gone horribly wrong for Lettice. There had been sex, there had been drugs, and now all the lifts home to Newtown that she was being offered involved both . . . So she'd cast herself adrift, got to a phone box and called Kemp, her guardian angel, her not-quite-uncle figure, who had raced to the rescue.

Even now he had to laugh. 'It was nearly closing time,' he said, 'but you had to go for a pee.'

Lettice didn't want to be reminded of that, so she raised her voice a semitone, and swept on. 'I'll meet you there in – what do they call it? The saloon bar. At eight o'clock. OK?'

'OK,' he agreed, weakly.

Mary would be wild; he wasn't too happy himself but he'd not had the strength to resist. I should have thought up a proper excuse earlier, he told himself, told her we were going away for the weekend – anything. Now it was too late. But at least he wasn't going to that awful flat.

He tried to put Lettice out of his mind, and succeeded by immersing himself in work that demanded concentration to rid himself of those over-night fears, and the terrible effect on him of that voice of hers – the one she could suddenly use to bring up the past.

Kemp didn't go straight home, however, when the office closed. He did what he had meant to do for some time.

He went to see Jim Sutherland, and in his pocket he had the diary of Dr Ayre for that essential date in August 1979.

He had got his timing right. This particular evening Marion would be out at her painting class, which would not finish until seven, and Jim would be at a loose end, perhaps watching the news, perhaps reading his journals. Lennox Kemp was a most welcome visitor.

'Don't seem to see the point these days of keeping up to date,' he said, leading Kemp into the sitting room. 'Time I took up something other than medicine. Once you're out of touch, you might just as well study astronomy. A drink?'

'No, thanks, I'm driving. You have your usual; it's that time of day,'

Jim sighed. 'If I'm not careful, it would always be that time of day. But I do normally have a quick gin at this time to brace myself for what awful announcements come at six o'clock out of the news. The National Health Service is rolling rapidly downhill with the private sector riding roughshod over everything we believed in back then in 1948. But I'm not going to bore you with my views on that. You've come here for summat. Out with it.'

Kemp took the small diary out of his pocket. 'On a hypothetical case, Jim, what would you say to a practitioner who altered the date of a patient's appointment for the record? For whatever reason, the date was altered so that the practitioner appeared not to have seen that patient for some months, whereas the original date showed he had been seen on a particular date. What could possibly be a reason for such an alteration being made on the patient's record?'

'How can you be certain such an alteration was made?

Kemp took out the notebook kept by Dr Ayre, and turned to the page in question. 'See, there's an obvious rubbing-out of a previous appointment, and then another entry made over it. Look through the diary, Jim. Dr Enid always saw her over-eighties on Tuesdays, this week she changed the entry to the Monday, which was the day she saw her private patients when they'd made appointments.'

Jim Sutherland skimmed through the pages of the diary. 'Much like the ones we always keep to carry about with us. Absolutely private, not part of any official record. I used to keep mine in the car when I was out doing visits, and I think Enid would do the same. What are you getting at, Lennox?'

'She altered the entries, Jim. In his statement to the police, Perce Cavendish said he had an appointment on Monday the thirteenth of August with Dr Ayre as a private patient at two thirty in the afternoon.'

Dr Sutherland sat back in his chair, and took a sip of the drink he had poured for himself. 'I'm beginning to remember something about this. Only dimly, I'm afraid, for it's over twenty years ago, but I was asked at the time if Cavendish was a patient of mine, and I said, no, he wasn't, he'd always been with Enid Ayre. He was a funny chap, Cavendish. We only met casually but when we did he seemed anxious to be friendly. He told me once that he was a foundling – a proper one, left on a doorstep – and brought up by two theatrical sisters around Covent Garden. They thought he was the by-blow of some chorus girl – well, that was possible. But when they died, he was left on his own, but some charity or other connected with the theatre meant he had some money. I think he was trying to tell me why he was a private patient of Enid's – when, in fact, it was no business of mine. Strange chap . . .'

'What do you think of Dr Ayre's alteration on that date?'

Jim Sutherland squinted at the page against the light of his reading lamp.

'There's no doubt it was changed. What did she say to the police? I presume they checked up on his alibi?'

'Not immediately. Dr Ayre was away on a three-week holiday.'

'So she was. I remember now. She'd told me she was taking one of these Hellenic cruises. She hadn't been on holiday in years. I'll say that for Enid, she was always punctilious about telling other practices when she'd be away. I told her it was time she took a break. What's the point you're trying to make?'

'Just that when she finally made a statement to the police, over three weeks had passed. And by then the prison doctor had been in touch with her and told her that Perce Cavendish had been suffering from stomach cancer for some months.'

'Ah, I see what you're getting at.' Jim Sutherland took time out to have long thoughts. At last he said, slowly, 'She would not like them to think she had seen this patient that Monday and had not made a proper examination which would have shown advanced cancer, something she had already missed.'

'Cavendish said she'd been treating him for peptic ulcer.'

'Hmm. Of course there are patients who don't tell their doctors the whole truth. Some underestimate the pains they have because they're scared. I just don't know, Lennox . . .'

He stopped and looked gravely across at Kemp. 'Just as I don't know what you're up to, but if it means trouble for someone, then, please, drop it. Both Marion and I have talked a lot about this story of the Aumarys, that you introduced liquor into the house of a known alcoholic, and we have decided that it's not true. Neither of us believes it. There may be some reason. I don't know this Miss Maitland, but all I can say is that she has been mistaken. Let's leave it like that, Lennox.'

'Well, thanks for your trust, you and Marion. As you know, I've been the subject of rumours in the past and they never bothered me. Now in my middle age I'm more sensitive, and I have a business to think of, not to mention Mary. But I've no wish to get this thing out of all proportion. I'm seeing Lettice at the end of the week before they leave for the States. I just wish they would be the ones to drop the story. But there's still something of the headstrong girl in her, she gets the bit between her teeth, and won't let go. As for Miss Maitland, there's bitterness there, but why she'd direct it at me I've no idea. Now I've taken up too much of your time.'

As they were going into the hall he said, 'I understand that Perce Cavendish did a drawing or a painting of young Dominic in the old Parish Hall. Did you ever see it?'

'Of course, everybody did round about the time the Primary School put on that little play. He'd done it in pastels, and Marion tells me it showed he had a lot of talent. The irony was that it had to be in that old building the police set up their crime unit when the boy went missing, and afterwards it was where they held the investigation into the murder. But of course when they'd arrested Cavendish the drawing had to go.' Jim Sutherland gave a wry smile. 'The Mothers' Union had their scrubbing brushes out in no time. A pity – I too thought it was good, he caught the elfin quality people said Dominic had.'

'A straight question, Jim: were you absolutely certain that Perce Cavendish was guilty of the murder?'

Sutherland thought for a moment. 'Nowadays paedophiles are news, they're even registered as such, so be warned . . . At the time I simply thought of Cavendish as being a bit of a loser, a piece of flotsam washed up here out of a theatrical world which was then springing up in Stratford – the London one – where he'd come from. He did have a way with kids – they flocked to his play-acting. But I didn't know the man, Lennox, so I really can't answer your question properly. There was sufficient evidence, the police were certain of his guilt – that had to be good enough for the rest of us. Had I known the poor devil was suffering from stomach cancer – well, I might not have spoken of him as harshly as I did. And when I look back now, and see more clearly, I can't help wondering how any man could have drawn that boy the way he did, then take him from his home and callously kill him.'

'You didn't know the mother?'

'No. She was on the list of the practice in Ember Village and so I didn't know either her or her son. As you can understand, Lennox, we were all horrified. We tend to think that murders happen elsewhere, never on our doorstep, and this was a thoroughly nasty one. One of the medicos told me that the small body had been thrown into that hedge like a bit of old rubbish, something someone had finished with . . .'

Kemp felt the shock of the words and knew they came from the old doctor's heart. For forty years Jim Sutherland had done his best to sustain the health and wellbeing of the people of Newtown, and in that time he had comforted many who were bereaved. But the death of Dominic Fenwick had been different; it would never be forgotten.

Twenty

For the rest of Kemp's week, Friday night effectively blotted out the future, sitting on his mind like a Brillo pad which he could neither think through nor get round. He felt as if he were back in student days with an exam looming, and all roads beyond it closed.

To defeat this shadow which was darkening his way forward he tried all manner of self-help: sweet reason (why should a simple meeting bulk so large?), humour (he had once found Lettice Warrender quite funny, why did she now seem so terrible?), careful analysis of the situation (she would have her say, he would respond, they would part, end of story) and, finally, when all this failed, he talked to his wife.

'You're nervous,' she said, as if diagnosing a new malady.

'I'm scared.'

'But why?'

'That's what I'm asking you. I want an objective, third-party view.'

'I won't be a third party in anything involving Lettice Aumary, and there's no way I can be objective about the one I love, and the father of my child.'

It got them both roaring with laughter, and lightened the moment, but it couldn't last.

'You tend to get obsessive about things,' said Mary, gravely because she had in these last few weeks become concerned about him. 'Since you met those people again you have been pulled back into the past, and the same goes for you finding the diaries of that doctor. Is there a connection?'

'Oh, yes, indeed there is. The way Lettice spat out those words about Cavendish, the forgetfulness of her husband, who was in Newtown at the time and must have known all about the case, and poor old Roger's reaction just to the name. And of course the combined Aumary animosity to me because of this wild tale of their Miss Maitland . . . The connection's there in my mind all right, but I can't somehow handle it properly.'

'You're not only dealing with their memories, you're dealing with your own,' said Mary, shrewdly. 'How well did you actually know them, twenty years ago? You talk about the Warrenders being gentry, and some people in the town resented it. More to the point, did you?'

'Good heavens, no. Why should I? I had plenty of other things to worry about at the time, getting back into my proper career after those six years out of the law, organizing my new office at Gillorns – people like the Warrenders weren't important to me.'

'Not even Lettice?'

'I liked the girl, she was spirited and bright. Looking back now, I can see that for me she provided light relief in those hard days; she amused me. Perhaps I should have taken her more seriously – or rather been more perceptive about her feelings for me.' He sighed. 'She was just at the age for hero-worship, straight out of books. She must have seen me as a figure to be saved, the outcast, the man who had blotted his copy-book, and needed redemption . . .'

Mary giggled. 'Even in those days your appearance wouldn't have helped you to look tragic, but Lettice may have been the kind of girl who collected slightly worn teddy bears . . . To be serious, though, if you have these nasty forebodings about Friday evening, why go?'

'It'll be unfinished business if I let them get away with it. And I do want to find out more about any link Roger had with Cavendish. That case still troubles me.'

'It's the boy, isn't it? The violence that was done to him.'

'And the attitude of people at the time. One can't blame them for not talking about it but they went on blotting it out of their minds – only the children really remembered, and their memories are faulty because they didn't really know what happened, so each would fill it in for themselves . . . Of course, I'd like to shake the whole thing out of my mind, but I can't . . .'

'If you think meeting Lettice is going to help you get it out of your mind, then I'm all for it. Will you just sit there and talk over the old times?'

The edge in Mary's voice told him that the discussion was over. She had not quite given her blessing to this Friday night rendezvous but at least she had listened.

Twenty years had passed lightly over the King's Head public house in Wanstead. It had moved with the times but the times had been good to it. It might have lost its old image as a staging post, a temporary stopping-off place for the coaches out of the City on the long road north but it had gained a more comfortable air of permanence. Now people not only came in for food and drink, they stayed, for it was still near to London but far cheaper than the hotels in the metropolis.

Kemp and Lettice arrived nearly together. He had decided to come in by train; it suited his mood for he was feeling reckless rather than abstemious and if she took umbrage early he could still have a good dinner himself, and take the late train home. He saw her paying off her taxi as he arrived after the ten-minute walk from the station, but he slipped in a side door without her seeing him, and secured a table in a corner of the saloon bar so that he could rise to his feet as she came in the door. He felt the manoeuvre gave him an advantage – at least initially.

She wore a high-necked emerald-green dress in some kind of woollen material under a camel-hair coat which she was slipping from her shoulders as she came towards him. Greeting him pleasantly if a trifle brusquely, she laid the coat tenderly to rest on the seat of the chair beside her as if it was a pet animal which had cost a lot.

Drinks were ordered, and he told her he had booked dinner for nine o'clock, a statement she accepted without comment. They talked about the weather, a little about his work and she remembered her manners sufficiently to ask after Mary and the child, though Kemp suspected she had already forgotten Elspeth's name in the way people do when they have no children of their own.

He was about to ask if she was enjoying her stay in London when he stopped himself; her brother's death would have vitiated any enjoyment she might have had on this trip. Instead he enquired about Tod's mission in Scotland. Tersely, she said that he would be back tomorrow, and they could leave the country next week if nothing further prevented them. Kemp thought she looked tired, but only observed, diplomatically, that going through Roger's effects must be wearisome for her. Did she have Miss Maitland's help?

Miss Maitland was dismissed in a few words. 'I don't know what's got into the woman,' said Lettice. 'All she can think of is getting to Australia as quickly as possible. She got into such a dither that Tod had to do most of the arrangements for her himself, even while he's busy. I thought she was a calm, sensible person but she's become jumpy as a cat on hot bricks, and not much help to me at all. We're going to leave everything in the hands of Tod's London solicitors, sell the flat and store the furniture for now. I would like to stay here to see to things being done prop-

163

erly, but Tod won't have it, and I can see why. My place is with him, and he needs me in New York, we have social obligations as well as his professional ones.'

This seemed to Kemp to be the kind of speech she was making to everyone, explaining herself in more detail than required. If there had been arguments about her return to the States, her husband had obviously won them.

By way of diversion, Kemp told her that he'd had a visit from Daniel Dempster. Lettice looked startled. 'What did he want with you?' she said, sharply.

'Well, for one thing, to knock me down for bringing Roger whisky. I had to tell him that tale was simply not true—'

'Miss Maitland had no reason to lie,' Lettice broke in. 'And there's no other explanation as to how it got into the downstairs bathroom.'

'Miss Maitland lied about a lot of things, including my original phone call that Friday afternoon. I'd still like to know why she did it, and if you're not going to tell me then I'll just have to find out on my own.'

'But that's ridiculous, there was nobody else there that day, and Miss Maitland wouldn't lie, not about something as important as that – you have to remember it was she who found Roger unconscious from the effects of that drink and the pills he'd swallowed. I wish you'd simply admit it, Lennox, it would make things so much easier for everyone. It was a stupid prank. I think you were trying to get your own back for what happened all those years ago between you and Roger . . . You had a grievance.'

Fortunately at that point they were approached by a waiter, who told them their table was ready; otherwise Kemp might have given Lettice the rough edge of his tongue. Anyway, she'd already knocked back two drinks, and was doing most of the talking. For the time being he would remain polite.

'That man Dempster,' she said, when they were seated, 'rather common, I thought. Torvil and I wondered if he was after money, but it seems all he wants are the letters he used to send to Roger when he was overseas. I said when I found them I would send them on to him.' She gave a little laugh. 'I've certainly no wish to read that kind of thing.'

'Oh, come off it, Lettice.' He nearly called her 'Lettie' but something in the folds of the green dress forbade him. 'Daniel Dempster seems a very decent man, and I think he did more for your brother than all those rehabs put together.'

It was the wrong thing to say. Despite the presence of a waiter at her elbow offering warm bread rolls, Lettice flared up like an outraged teenager (after all, it hadn't been so long since her forbears looked on servants as unpolished bits of the furniture). 'My husband, as a doctor, knew better than any hick seaman from nowhere as to how my brother should be treated.'

'But look at the result of his ministrations,' said Kemp, spreading his hands, eloquently. He was being unnecessarily cruel but he found Lettice at her worst when she was snobbish. 'Roger might have been better off left to his friend, Daniel. I think that man really loved him.'

'We all loved him.' It was proclaimed like a reading from the gospel. 'How dare you put a family who loved and cared for Roger in the same category as that hunk of a seaman?'

Fortunately, at that point the menu had to be scrutinized, which, for the minute, put a stop to their conversational combat. Kemp found Lettice as quickly selective on food as she was with the topics she considered worthy of attention. She ordered her meal as smartly as she dismissed Daniel Dempster, but Kemp was determined to pursue the subject.

'All I meant to say was that Dempster seemed to me to be a good friend at a time when Roger needed one. After all, you hadn't seen your brother in years.'

'I relied on Torvil to keep an eye on him. He'd always done that. They were brought up together, as you know, and right through prep school, and when they were at Rugby, it was Torvil who looked after him.'

'You're implying that he considered Roger as the weaker of the two?'

Lettice spluttered into her soup spoon. 'Why do you always have to say such hateful things? You've always had a down on both of them. And I know why,' she ended, triumphantly, taking up the last of her soup and exactly placing her spoon in correct position in the empty bowl. 'You've never forgiven them for that schoolboy prank of theirs.'

'Schoolboy prank? They broke my arm.'

She was shaken. 'I didn't know that . . .' she said.

'No, I bet they wouldn't tell you,' he said, quietly, determined not to let her off the hook now that she had raised the subject. 'Nor how they laid a trap for me by arranging an appointment through my office which brought me out to the old Halstead Manor property. They wouldn't tell you that once they'd knocked me down, they cracked my elbow with a wooden stave, and then kicked me senseless. A schoolboy prank? I don't think so, Lettice. One of them was already a doctor . . . The violence they meted out to me was equal to anything the Roding lads were capable of. Council-estate louts, they called them. Well, how do you tell the difference?'

He hadn't meant to say so much but he'd already had a few drinks himself, her attitude was irritating him beyond measure, and suddenly the memory – something he must have suppressed for years – came so close he could feel the same outrage and pain as he'd felt then. Besides, what had been her viewpoint once she'd been told – a romantic one, two knights protecting her honour? Well, it was time she grew up.

Seeing her stunned into silence, but hiding her discomfiture in a scrutiny of the vegetable dishes, he finished: 'I'm sorry, Lettice, but on that evening nearly twenty years ago, your kin meant business, savage business.'

He helped himself to potatoes, feeling shaken by memories he had hoped long erased. But of course his disclosure had given her an advantage, which she promptly picked up.

'I can understand, Lennox. It must have been a bad experience, and I can see why you have held against both Torvil and Roger ever since. And you took the chance to get your revenge on my poor brother . . . Yes, I can understand it, but I still think bringing him that bottle of whisky was a beastly way to go about it.'

She now adjusted her fully laden plate, and commenced to chomp through the food as she used to do as a girl when he would take her to lunch at the Cabbage White public house in Newtown.

She still had the power to take his breath away, and it was some time before he could regain sufficient to continue the conversation. 'I didn't ask to come back into the lives of you and your brother. If you'll remember, it was you who pleaded with me to visit him because he wanted to see me. And I never found out why.'

'I thought it was obvious.' She took care to swallow the whole mouthful like a good little girl, before she spoke. 'He wanted to apologize to you for that incident. Jolly brave of him, really.'

Her idea, that Roger Warrender had played the perfect English gentleman right to the end, forgiving his enemies and showing contrition towards those he might have harmed, was too much for Kemp. He gave his full attention to his steak, and said nothing, which enabled her to continue in gentle mode.

'And we should emulate him, Lennox. Forgive and forget. I am quite prepared to put aside your foolish

167

behaviour at the flat. I would like to return to the States with a better remembrance of you, and forget how you've let me down . . .'

Fortunately, the chef in the kitchens of the King's Head was a dab hand with fillet steak and Kemp's was quite memorable, otherwise Lettice Aumary might have got it all over her forgiving face. Only when he had done justice to the dish in front of him did he return to the fray.

'You can't forgive someone for a sin which was never committed. I shall make it my business, by means legal or otherwise, to find out just why your Miss Maitland lied. But now I'm going to change to another subject.'

Lettice was looking down her nose at her portion of sea bass, which deserved more in the way of appreciation.

'Very well,' she said, 'we'll leave that matter for the moment. What is your new subject?'

'How close was your brother to the man, Perce Cavendish?'

Lettice jabbed her fork into the poor fish with such force that she split the skin and flesh through to the bone. An unbecoming crimson colour spread down her neck to clash vividly with the high collar of her dress, and it took a few minutes for her to recover enough to speak.

'Why must you always bring up the most awful things to talk about? What on earth did that horrible man have to do with us?'

'You remember the case?'

'No, I don't. I just know he was a very nasty man, a pervert, and he killed that lovely little boy. We weren't even there when it happened.'

'Who's we?'

'Myself, and Pa and Ma. We were all in France that August.'

'You seem very sure. Why do you remember it?

'Because that August – 1979 – I was waiting for the

results of my degree exams. I was being nervy and difficult, I suppose, so Pa thought I'd be better going abroad
during that awful waiting time.' She paused. 'He was more
perceptive than I'd given him credit for. Anyway, we took
a house in Brittany.'

'And you all went? Including Roger?'

'No, Roger stayed at home. He'd failed to get into the
Oxford College he'd been intended for, so he had to study
for entrance to the Business School. Even in those days
Roger was no scholar.'

'So, he was left at Castleton House. On his own?'

Lettice frowned, as if trying to discover hidden meaning
in Kemp's words.

'Well, Torvil was always around. He was doing his regis-
trarship at the North Mid that summer, and he'd pop over
whenever he had time off.'

'You still haven't answered my question, Lettice. How
close was Roger to Perce Cavendish?'

She'd had time to go through things in her head; all this
talk of exams and studying for them, the holiday in France,
she was putting up a smokescreen. Now she became petulant.

'You've been listening to all those horrible rumours that
were going about. I'd thought you were above that kind of
gossip.'

'What kind of gossip? I wasn't in Newtown then.'

The arrival of tempting delights on the sweets trolley gave
her time to compose a suitable answer. She waited until the
waiter had gone.

Dipping her spoon into something artfully constructed
out of the sort of chocolate an Aztec king might have had
laid before him, she said, 'At that time there had been some
hostility towards us in Newtown because we had sold some
of our land to a property developer – and not to the Council.
It hadn't made us popular.'

Here she was going all round the houses again – in this case not only figuratively. He would have to stop her.

'I'm only interested in Perce Cavendish.'

'I know you are,' she said, with a show of temper. 'Ever since that dinner at the Sutherlands, you keep on about him. He's dead – and a good thing too, after what he did to that boy.'

'Had he been a friend of Roger's?'

'I wouldn't have called him a friend. He was a bad influence on my brother.'

'In what way?'

'He encouraged him to be . . . He just wasn't a suitable person for Roger to have as a friend. It wasn't normal . . .'

'Oh, spit it out, Lettice. They were both gay.' Seeing the red colour rise in her face, he continued, more gently. 'It's not going to harm Roger now by admitting it. Anyway, I think you've always known.'

'I didn't understand. Ma would never speak about it, she was too ashamed. It was Torvil who told me, and he was very understanding. He'd always looked after Roger, which meant seeing he didn't get into the wrong company, but, well, Roger could be difficult.'

'And Roger went on seeing Perce Cavendish?'

'It was that play they put on for the kids. Roger got involved, helped with the scenery and the rehearsals. Ma was furious – it took him right away from the studying he was supposed to be doing that summer.' Lettice didn't look too displeased at this aspect, and Kemp surmised that Paula hadn't got much sympathy from her daughter over Roger's wasted time. 'I think Roger was rather taken up by the theatrical side of Cavendish – even I could see why he was attracted to him though I didn't like the man.'

'Roger must have been devasted when it happened, the murder, I mean.'

'As I told you, we weren't there. Torvil had to cope with

that. We didn't return till the end of August, and by then Cavendish was in prison. I remember there was a terrible scene at Castleton because Roger wanted to go and visit him. Can you imagine? Of course Father put his foot down, something he didn't do very often but when he did you knew you had to obey him.'

'Roger went out on the police search when the boy was missing. He offered because he knew the countryside, and had a car.'

'It was Torvil who went out to help look for the boy, along with others from Castleton House. He told me that, later. He thought it was the least they could do. I don't know whether Roger went with him or not, but I know he used Roger's old car. He said if he'd used his own people would think he was showing off. That was typical of Torvil, even then. He was always aware of the feelings of others.'

Lettice continued to talk of her husband in what could only be called glowing terms, and totally without either humour or irony, until coffee was brought. They had asked for it to be brought to their table rather than go into the lounge, which Lettice said 'was noisy and full of people'. Kemp wondered if she would have preferred goldfish, and was surprised she had not said 'common people'. Her mother would have done so.

The topic, however, did give him the opportunity he'd been waiting for, almost since their first meeting at the Sutherlands' dinner table. Why had she married her cousin? Now he managed to insert the question into the conversation without it seeming impertinent.

She took her usual long way round to answer it. 'You remember you came out to Castleton House on some legal business for my grandmother – making her will, I think it was?'

'Yes,' said Kemp, cautiously, 'I remember.'

'That was when I began to get a schoolgirl crush on you, Lennox.'

This, to Kemp, had become rather embarrassing, and he began to wish he'd never asked about her marriage. She had drunk a great deal more of the two bottles of wine than he had, and the effect was to loosen her tongue. He made a great fuss of pouring coffee, and fiddling with cups and saucers, rather to the surprise of the waiter standing by. But nothing could stop Lettice now. She spoke in a low tone as if still guarding her maiden self while she spoke of her passion for him, how he had evoked her pity – always a dangerous emotion in a young girl who had hitherto squandered it on dogs or ponies – and finally her love.

'But I was sure you thought of me as an uncle figure,' said Kemp, trying to lighten the matter.

'You made me your confidante, which was so brave of you, I thought, and I stood up for you when people talked about you being thrown out of the Law Society.'

'This is old history, Lettice, and best left that way.'

'I'm telling you because you asked why I married Torvil. Well, after a while I began to see that I hadn't a hope of getting you to love me. That you thought of me in quite a different way, as you say, like a niece. I came to my senses, but it was pretty miserable, I can tell you. Used to cry into my pillow for hours . . .'

Kemp began to wish himself anywhere but in the restaurant of the King's Head. He concentrated on his coffee cup, and looked forward to going home.

Twenty-One

Eventually Kemp was indeed at home, and much earlier than he had expected. After he had ordered a fresh pot of coffee, and Lettice had taken him slowly through more of her early years, she had quite suddenly announced that she'd had too much to drink and would he please get her a taxi.

She spoke with care, leaving sufficient space between the words so as not to slur them, and her exit from the restaurant was with dignity and a proper sense of direction. She briefly visited the ladies' room, and emerged wrapped in her expensive coat, her hair freshly combed. She leaned a little on Kemp's arm as he led her to an armchair in the lounge. 'You'll think I'm like my brother,' she said, giggling a little, but he assured her that such an idea would never cross his mind.

While they waited for her cab, she talked again about Roger. 'He tried to play the young man about town, but he hadn't the money. He tried to be a businessman, but he hadn't the brains. What was there left? Torvil was marvellous over the years, the way he kept propping him up. Without him, I think Roger would have died years ago. He'd had breakdowns, of course, but we didn't talk about them at home. Even that summer, the one you keep going on about, Roger had some kind of nervous illness. The family said it was worry over his exams that brought it on . . . But I don't know . . .'

By the time Kemp had put Lettice into her taxi, and refused a lift to the station, he felt he had been through a three-decker novel, the chronicle of the Warrenders, and he was exhausted. The walk to the train helped clear his head, and he arrived home in a better frame of mind than when he'd left.

This was obvious to Mary, who sat with him now as he tried to explain what the evening had been like.

'It all sounds so cosy,' she said, sceptically, 'except for her confession of unrequited love. I don't want to say I told you so, but . . .'

'Yes, you did tell me that was the trouble with Lettice. I simply hadn't realized it had gone so deep. And, no, she didn't apologize for Miss Maitland, and retracted nothing of her tale. That lady is off to Australia tomorrow, and Lettice will probably go with her to Heathrow. The Aumarys will travel back to the States sometime next week.'

'And that's all?' Mary stared at him, wide-eyed. 'After all the fuss you made, the forebodings, the fear, your reluctance to even meet the woman . . . The two of you have a cosy chat about old times, then goodbye, and she's away!'

'Bit of an anticlimax, I admit.' And that was exactly how he was feeling; it was as if he'd lost the fight, or Lettice had talked him out of any desire for one. And yet . . .

'Did you kiss her farewell as you put her in her taxi? I love that expression – it has an old-world ring, as if the lady was being helped into her carriage and a rug spread over her delicate knees. Well, did you give her a kiss to remember you by?'

'As a matter of fact it was she who did the kissing – a cool one on my cheek. I think it was meant to signal forgiveness for my shortcomings. Once again in her life I had failed her.'

Mary gave a little snort. 'I'm glad to hear it. I'm damned if I would allow any flare-up of that girlish passion, and I'm not sure you'd be safe to play uncle.'

'It wouldn't have been difficult,' said Kemp, blandly. 'She'd put away a fair amount of wine, but the seduction of an American matron wasn't what I had in mind.'

Mary regarded him warily. 'I think you got what you wanted – with a little help from the drink. You wanted to get Lettice talking. The bit about her marriage was interesting.'

'That Torvil wasn't her cousin? Everyone thought that the fair Giselle – her of the greyhound legs – was his mother, but apparently not. She couldn't have children, so she and Richard adopted an American boy who'd been orphaned in a plane crash. The parents had been friends of the Aumarys. He was only a baby at the time, and they gave him everything including a new name with an old ancestral twist to it.'

'Torvil-Tod seems to find changing a name as simple as changing your socks. But I can see how your Lettice was attracted to him – once she'd got over her love of teddy bears, of course.'

Kemp ignored the jab. He was more concerned with his own ambivalent feelings towards Aumary, and he was trying to sort them out as he spoke.

'The adopted boy did well, turned out to be a wunderkind, then an industrious student, a successful career doctor – and to crown all, the finest husband in the world.'

'Do I hear the rattle of sour grapes, my darling?'

'You'd have to dry them before they'd rattle . . .' Under the light words Kemp was still examining his own view of Torvil Aumary, and he was not liking what he found. The more Lettice had eulogized her husband, as she had done tonight, the more Kemp became aware of growing resentment. It was like having a professional colleague praised to your face for qualities you'd never noticed he had. It wasn't the high position Torvil had reached in his vocation which rankled – the road he had chosen in the global field of medicine could not have been easy to achieve, and Kemp would not grudge him his success. No, what was bothering Kemp in a nasty way deep down in his own psyche was that Torvil had turned out to be such a super husband!

Mary interrupted this troublesome thought by remarking that she had assumed the Aumarys didn't have children because they'd been cousins when they married. As that was not the case, had Lettice in her intimate disclosures given any reason for their childlessness?

'No, she didn't but I think babies were sacrificed in the interests of Torvil's career. It didn't seem to worry Lettice, in fact she said they'd never really wanted a family.'

'Perhaps her own had proved too much for her. I wonder why Torvil took such an interest in brother Roger.'

'Oh, I think that was pressure of family. The Warrenders at Castleton House doted on the boy Torvil, the brilliant scholar, the hard-worker – everything that poor Roger was not. Perhaps they thought his good qualities would rub off on their own son. What is more surprising to me is that he kept it up, despite his workload. Looking after Roger seems to have been a priority.'

'And there's no doubt that Torvil isn't gay – even meeting him just the once I know that. Actually, he is a very attractive man – I told you that after the dinner party.'

'Well, don't tell me again. I'm sick of hearing about how wonderful he is, you don't need to throw in good looks as well.' Acknowledging that he sounded just a trifle petulant, he added: 'I think it's time we were in bed.'

Saturday for the Kemps was a treasured time; morning meant yawns, late breakfast, romps with Elspeth, afternoon too was devoted to the child – latecomer in two bleak lives – with games in the garden or long walks in her pushchair, while the evening sprawled out in delicious leisure for bath-time, bed and story-telling.

This particular autumn Saturday afternoon was calm and sunny, so they went to the park, the old Victorian one in the centre of Newtown, not the new highly structured area at the Leisure Centre. The slides and swings might be old-fashioned but the place was quiet, the overgrown lanes peaceful. Walking slowly back home, they didn't talk much, but both their thoughts were on the child, and the difference her innocent presence made to everything.

It was six o'clock in the evening and Kemp was covered in soap suds when Mary came into the bathroom, her face grave.

'It's Tod Aumary on the phone. He sounds worried. I'll take over in here.'

Downstairs, Kemp lifted the receiver, brushing soapy froth from his shirt.

'What is it, Dr Aumary?'

'Kemp, thank God you're there. I have to ask you to come out to the flat at once. It's Lettice – she's in a bad way.'

'What do you mean?'

'It's serious – I wouldn't ask you if it wasn't. She must see you. She has something terrible to tell you. Something's she's just found out. I sorry, I can't say more on the phone. Please come.'

Kemp was shaking his head. 'What is it about? Why should Lettice want to see me? What good can I do?'

Aumary's voice rose, unlike his usual level tone. 'I'm in despair, Kemp . . . Please . . . She needs you. I can't do anything.'

A second's pause.

'All right, I'll come.'

He put down the phone, and went slowly upstairs. Mary was in the nursery, slipping a tired little girl under the jungle animals on the duvet. She finished tucking her in before she turned.

'He wants me there at the flat. Something has happened to Lettice.'

'Don't go.' Mary leaned over and kissed Elspeth's forehead, smoothing back the damp hair. 'Don't go,' she said again. Then, to the child: 'Back in a minute, pet, and Mummy will read you a story.'

On the landing she faced him.

'I don't care if Lettice Aumary is on her deathbed, you're not to go.'

'I have to, Mary. She's asked for me. Her husband sounds desperate. All he could say was that she has found out something terrible, and she must tell me. She needs me . . .'

'We need you, Lennox.' But she knew he wouldn't understand. She felt as if her whole soul was taking flight, but it was no use, she would just have to be practical. 'Anyway, I think you know very well what she's got to say. Her brother was involved in the murder of that little boy . . . You've known that for some time, haven't you?'

'Yes, I've known in a sketchy kind of way. I think she must have found out something when she's been going through Roger's things. It would have a terrible effect on her.'

'I don't care.' Mary met his eyes steadily, her face like stone. 'You must not go,' she said, again.

But he turned away. She put a hand on her heart as if to calm its fierce beating, and went back to the nursery.

Kemp tried not to think at all on his journey to Wanstead, concentrating on the traffic and the time. Between the end of afternoon activities and evening pleasures, the streets were quieter than on week days and he drove up the little drive to the flat just before seven. The lamp shone haltingly amber and red, swinging in the wind as he pulled the bell chain.

It was Dr Aumary who opened the door. 'Thank God

you're here, Kemp,' was all he said as he ushered him in and closed the heavy door behind him. 'Leave your coat on the chair.' It seemed the routine of the house, Kemp thought, as he pulled his arms out of the sleeves.

He had no further thoughts for some time, only the instant, blinding pain of a blow on the back of his head – then, nothing.

There was a light shining behind his eyelids, then a shadow moved across it and he heard someone say: 'Ah, you're coming round. Good. I didn't want to hit you too hard.'

Kemp managed to open his eyes. Torvil Aumary was standing above him, and they were both in the green-and-gold sitting room at the flat. There was pain at the back of his head and he put up a hand to feel the place. At least that's what his brain directed him to do except that the hand wouldn't obey the instruction. Without moving his head too much – instinct told him that would hurt – he glanced down and saw that both wrists were firmly bound to the arms of his chair, the one Roger had sat in. The chair's upholstery ended in two pieces of carved mahogany and it was to these his hands were tied with straps that looked as if they were off some sports equipment, only light straps but sufficient for their purpose.

He was making these observations separately from the more pertinent thoughts going through his mind. He was thankful that, although the blow to the back of his head had been heavy enough to knock him out, it didn't seem to have interfered with his power to think. He wondered about time, and found that by looking down again he could just make out the hands on his watch. It was eight o'clock. Relieved to find that he hadn't lost too many hours out of his life, he tried his voice and discovered that it worked.

'I should have guessed,' he said. 'Where's Lettice?'

Aumary, who had been strolling up and down the room,

came back and stood over him. 'Oh, didn't she tell you last night? She's taken Millie to Heathrow. Then she's going straight back to the hotel, so I'm afraid she's not coming to your rescue.'

'I thought it was supposed to be the other way round. I don't suppose she even knows I'm here.'

Torvil drew up a chair beside Kemp, and sat down. He had a small gun in his hand, which he slipped into his pocket. 'That's for later,' he said. 'No, Lettice doesn't know but she'll be appalled to learn of your suicide and the cause of it. Of course, like everyone else she'll put it down to your depression after you caused the death of her brother. People are funny, you know, they'll believe anything if you say it enough times.'

'Your Miss Maitland's a good example,' said Kemp, grimly. 'She was probably starting to believe her story was true. How'd you get her to do it? Money?'

'Not entirely. I had found a small flaw in her qualifications – or rather the lack of them. She'd never actually made it as a nurse but pretended she had. And, of course, she'd do anything for the Warrender family. Where would we be without our faithful old retainers? She watched over Roger for me, and kept in touch with me by phone. That's how I knew you were about to visit that Friday afternoon, and I had the idea I could use you . . .'

'Why?'

'Because you had become a great nuisance, old chap. Too inquisitive by half. And talking to my Lettice. Well, I had to put a stop to that. What with poor Roger wanting to spill it all before he killed himself, and to you of all people! I had to do something to split you all up, you and Lettice, you and Roger . . . After all the years I'd managed to keep him quiet. He wouldn't talk then of course because he was involved as much as I was . . .'

'In the death of Rickie Fenwick?'

Torvil was looking at his watch. 'Haven't got all night, old man, to talk about such things. I've got an alibi to set up. I'm on the night train from Edinburgh, gets in to King's Cross in an hour or so. I'll be phoning Lettice from the train and asking her to meet me, so you see I've got to be at the station before then.'

Kemp shifted his position as best he could and wondered how he was going to get out of this. He wasn't optimistic. He'd tried to move his legs and found that they too were securely fastened.

Torvil was watching him. 'Those straps aren't very tight because I don't want any marks to show up at the post-mortem. I've seen just how the suicide angle can work – I had to follow a case in New York once where it was done successfully, so I know how to do it down to the last detail. Do you want to hear about it?'

'No, I'll take your word for it. I'd rather hear about Rickie Fenwick.'

'Dear me, you are obsessed about that boy. Do you know that over the years I'd almost forgotten him. Not like Roger, he remembered all right, and when Lettice told him you'd brought the thing up at the Sutherlands, well, all he wanted was to tell you the full story – and then put out the light himself.'

'Which of you actually did it?'

Dr Aumary settled himself in his chair, cradling the gun in his lap. 'Well, I'll keep it short. I do hate those long explanations in the last chapters of books, don't you? All that happened was Roger and I were out in my new Ferrari, when we passed the Fenwick place. There was the youngster in the garden, and Roger shouts: "Like a spin?" and of course he comes running. We end up out at Castleton House, and have a bit of fun chasing the boy all over the house, which we had to ourselves anyway. I'd gone down to the kitchen, I think, in search of something to eat when I heard the screaming. Roger had got carried away. He'd gone too far. I raced upstairs and found him trying to stop the screams by stuffing socks in the boy's mouth. But it was far, far too late. He'd realized what was going on, and he was struggling. And the terrible shrieking . . . Well, I knew we'd had it. The place was empty, the family away, but there were always servants about, and there was a gardener on the terrace below the window.' Aumary paused. 'I've never looked back till now. It was over in an instant. Boys' necks are very tender, you know. It had to be done otherwise Roger and I were lost. We kept the body at Castleton, and on my insistence, we joined in the search using Roger's old car. Then the next night – or it might have been the one after, I've forgotten exactly when – I was going back to London so I took the body and chucked it over a hedge. Then I put the whole thing out of my mind, and advised Roger to do the same.'

'And the boy's shoes?'

'Good Lord, I'd quite forgotten that part. While we were out on that search I put them in Perce Cavendish's van. Roger was furious but I thought it was brilliant. The idea was to send the coppers off on a wild goose chase. Incidentally, in case you're thinking me the most awful beast, I'd already guessed that Perce had carcinoma of the stomach – he was always complaining about the pains and I recognized the symptoms even if that old lady quack thought it was an ulcer.'

'It doesn't excuse you for what happened.' Kemp felt very tired, and wished the whole thing would end.

As if in response to that wish, Dr Aumary got up and leaned over him. 'This is the spot,' he said, as if explaining something to a patient, 'just behind the ear. I'm sorry, I can't go on with our conversation but once you've gone I've got quite a lot of things to do to arrange the scene.'

'At least Roger Warrender got a drop of whisky to see him off,' Kemp murmured.

'Sorry I can't manage that,' said the doctor. 'We're right out of the stuff. That was a neat trick, was it not? I only needed to fly down from Edinburgh when I heard you'd been. I came in the back way and planted the bottle where I knew good old Roger would find it. Nobody saw me and I was back in the Athens of the North the next morning, ready to come down by train with Lettice. She's a very trusting soul, is Lettice, and knows absolutely nothing about my schedule. That bottle worried you, I could see . . . But don't blame me for Roger's death, he was on the way out anyway, I just had to make sure he wasn't going to confess his sins first. And what could be a pleasanter end than hooch and painkillers?'

'You could try it on me,' said Kemp, fidgeting.

'Far too suspicious. Lightning never strikes and all that. Anyway, now I found this little gem among Roger's possessions . . . Probably given to him by that hulk of a seaman for protection in those dodgy dives they used to frequent. Of course, back in the States we've all become experts on firearms, and when I study something I do it properly.'

Kemp could well believe it. The hands now bringing the gun up were steady, as those of a good doctor should be. This time it wasn't fingers that stroked the back of his head but the cold rim of the gun barrel. He wanted to close his eyes – it seemed appropriate – but instead he found himself staring at a movement in the distance. He heard the dry click of the safety catch. There was a moment's pause, followed by a crash as a huge figure seemed to come flying down from the ceiling.

Then there was a loud explosion close to his ear, then silence . . . And nothing . . .

Twenty-Two

'I only went there for my letters,' said Daniel Dempster to Mary as they sat in the waiting room of the Intensive Care Unit at Whipps Cross Hospital. 'She told me she'd send them but she never did, and my sailing date was close. I always had a key to that garden door . . . I only wanted my letters.'

'You were sent by God,' said Mary, who was convinced of this.

He nodded. Nights of stars and days of storm had kept his mind open to the existence of all faiths.

'At first I thought the doctor was examining a patient in that chair. Then I saw the straps and the gun.' Dempster was no stranger to scenes of incipient violence no matter how bizarre, nor was the glimpse of a firearm enough to put him off; he'd broken up many a brawl, and taken guns away from stronger men than Tod Aumary. Dempster had simply launched himself across the floor despite that finger about to press the trigger.

'You saved him, Daniel,' Mary said now. The police had told her all they knew and how efficient Dempster had been with phone calls once he'd knocked Aumary out cold on the carpet. First, for an ambulance, then for the police themselves. In the meantime he'd showed commendable resource, removing the straps holding the figure bleeding in the chair, laying him down and using first aid, finally tearing up his own shirt to staunch the blood pouring from the victim's chest. The paramedics had been impressed as they got Kemp into the ambulance on his way to hospital – and emergency surgery.

'If only I'd got there sooner,' said Daniel, 'before that bullet got fired.'

'But it was deflected, the surgeon said, and tore across the top of his chest. Oh, Daniel, it missed his heart by a whisper!'

'Has he a chance, Mrs Kemp?'

She could not answer that for she did not know.

The hours were passing slowly. 'You should go home, Daniel,' she said, handing him a coffee at one in the morning.

'No. I must see it through.'

Finally, two doctors came in.

'We got that bullet out, Mrs Kemp, but he's lost a lot of blood, and is still unconscious.'

The other man was more senior. 'Go in and sit with him,' he said. 'We think he may have a fifty-fifty chance but of course we can't guarantee even that. Just keep on talking to him. Can you do that?'

'Oh, I can do that all right.' She turned to Dempster and told him again to go home.

He shook his head. 'I'll stick it out,' he said.

Mary stood beside her husband's bed. He's wired up, she thought, like the back of a television set. The sister hovering round the array of tubes and life-saving equipment said again, 'Talk to him. Just hold his hand and talk to him. It often works. It doesn't matter what you say, just talk, it's the voice that gets through.'

Mary took the chair by the bed and picked up the flaccid hand. She spread out the fingers. She was aware of the nurse fading into the background. Mary didn't care. She had a lot to say. In a low, level tone she began to tell him exactly what was on her mind.

'This has been your last case, Lennox Kemp. Even if God spares you – which I pray to Him that He does – I shall see to it that you never do this kind of thing ever again. Who do you think you are, gallivanting about trying to solve old murders? And you with a wife and baby daughter! You didn't think of them when you went dashing off on a curiosity binge. You abandoned us today – or was it yesterday now? – when you took no notice of warnings and raced off like any dumb hero to rescue a worthless woman. You should have listened to me, you should have listened to your own fears, they were real enough, but, oh no, you knew best. And that telephone call! You should have had more sense, Lennox Kemp, than to listen to the voice of the one you knew in your heart was guilty. Had you forgotten the flash of red old Granny Wheatcroft saw? The sun on a red Ferrari, and only one person could have been at the wheel.'

Mary moved in closer. 'The thing is, you've lost your touch. It's high time you paid attention to the things that matter in your life – myself and Elspeth – and stopped trying to be a private eye, a book detective, the romantic figure Lettice Warrender fell for all those years ago. If you get out of this, Lennox Kemp, I swear I'll never again let you out of my sight. You can go to the office and do all those dull things that lawyers do, but at six o'clock you'll come home to me and my daughter like an ordinary husband. Do you hear me, Lennox Kemp, this has been your last case.'

Mary sank back in her chair, exhausted. She almost let his hand slide from her grip and could scarcely believe in the tiny flicker of the fingers. She looked at his face and saw his eyes were opening. She lent over him, felt the small hiss of his breath.

'I heard your voice, Mary, so I knew I hadn't gone to heaven.'